CROOKED
V.1

EDITED BY
JESSIE KWAK

©2021 Jessie Kwak Creative LLC and the respective contributors.

EDITOR

Jessie Kwak

COVER IMAGE

By Vitalik Radko via Deposit Photos

ORNAMENTAL BREAK

Elements by Freepik and Good Ware from www.flaticon.com.

PUBLISHER

Bad Intentions Press

Portland, OR, USA

All rights reserved.

No part of this book may be reproduced in any form or by any electronic or mechanical means, including information storage and retrieval systems, without written permission from the author, except for the use of brief quotations in a book review.

For more information, please visit: jessiekwak.com/crooked

I grew up reading science fiction and fantasy. I write science fiction. But my true love is crime novels.

I love the fast pacing, the mystery, the cat-and-mouse play between the good guys and the bad guys. The heists, the cons, the double-crosses, the easy money jobs gone wrong — I love it all. When a crime story is set in our mundane world, it's fine.

But when it's set in a science fictional word? It lights me up.

You can find sci-fi crime stories scattered amid "first contact with alien" stories and "space marines defending galaxy-spanning empires" stories on the Science Fiction shelf. But — like the shifty criminals who lurk on their pages — sci-fi crime stories can be hard to nail down. They dance between categories, classified as "adventure" or "cyberpunk" or "general."

For years, I've been wanting to create a place for these misfits. A virtual Continental Hotel, the neutral territory where stories of space pirates, mobsters, private eyes, grifters, mercenaries, and lawmen can all hang up their

EVA suits and holster their blasters and share a whiskey in uneasy peace.

A place where readers who love both science fiction and crime stories can go to find their next thrilling read.

The book you're holding in your hands is the first step. When I first started talking about this anthology, Mark Teppo dubbed it the "Kwak wants more space heists" project — and he was one hundred percent correct.

Welcome to *Crooked*, the first volume of a new anthology series from Bad Intentions Press.

You'll find Teppo's retrieval job gone very, very wrong (or has it?). You'll find Eric Warren's gunrunner getting a second chance, Greg Dragon's smuggler surviving on the edge, Kate Sheeran Swed's unlikely bounty hunter getting her feet underneath her, and Wade Peterson's fighting bot showing its fiercely loyal heart.

The law is represented in this collection, too — you'll find Benjamin Gorman's take on an interspecies police investigation and Mark Niemann-Ross's story of near-future intellectual property noir.

And I snuck a story in, too — the very first one I'm releasing from my next series of space pirate shenanigans.

The goal of the *Crooked* anthology series is to introduce you, the reader, to authors who are currently writing sci-fi crime stories. Many of the short stories in this collection are set in larger universes, which means that if you read something you like, you'll find plenty more stories to keep you busy.

Find a new author you love? Follow the links at the end of each story for even more stories from the seedy underbelly of the Science Fiction shelf.

And if you want even more sci-fi crime in your life, head to jessiekwak.com/bad-intentions

Have fun out there,

Jessie Kwak

October 12, 2021

THE DOUBLEDEALER

AN INFINITY'S END SHORT STORY

BY ERIC WARREN

IT WAS A TRAP, THAT MUCH WAS OBVIOUS.

As Kave stood at the entrance to the alleyway, he could already tell Jergun wanted to meet him here because there was only one way in and out. The alley dead-ended at some discarded matter recyclers and a wall that reached thirty meters into the sky, matching the other buildings around it. Jergun wasn't here yet, giving Kave the impression she either wasn't going to show at all, or she was just waiting until her prey was in position. He half considered not even going in, but he hadn't gotten in this business to be soft.

What did Jergun think this was, amateur hour?

"You seeing this, Arex?" Kave asked into the subdermal comm he'd embedded in his jaw. It allowed him to speak to his ship with barely more than a whisper and was the next-best thing to telepathy. But no way was he letting anyone go in and mess around with his brain with one of those new internal transmitters; this was close enough.

"Affirmative, sir. It seems to be primed for a snare," the computer replied in his ear. Arex had what Kave called a flair for stating the obvious.

"Gimmie a multi-spread, within ten meters of my location, tight beam. And keep an eye on my life signs."

"As always, sir," the machine replied.

Kave sighed and walked into the alley, keeping his head down while at the same time checking his periphery. The alley was wide enough for six people to walk shoulder-to-shoulder, six humans at least, but with so much trash only two or three could reasonably manage to make it. Rotten yaarn and moogar wafted up from some of the piles, turning his nose. There were also no side exits, only a few maintenance doors to the buildings which enclosed the alleyway. Kave found an unobstructed part of the wall and melted into the darkness, his eyes focused on the entrance to the alley.

Less than two minutes later, a dark figure appeared at the opening. It stood there a moment, a black silhouette against the light from the main street before making its way in. The figure was tall, the shape fitting for a Karkurian. It was her, all right. Kave didn't move other than to place his free hand on the weapon hidden under his coat. The other figure stopped and pulled its hood back, revealing dark grey skin and almond-shaped black eyes.

Jergun.

She scanned the alley, apparently not seeing him in the darkness before she checked her comm. Kave pushed away from the wall and cleared his throat, his hand still on the weapon.

Jergun flinched at the sound, then dropped her arms. "You're here."

Kave motioned to the walls around them without taking his eyes off her. "Nice meeting place."

"It suits my needs," she replied. "Shall we get on with it? Or do humans like to stall?"

He'd never dealt with this Karkurian before but had plenty of experience with the species. Most were blunt, rude, and cared little for species not their own. This one seemed no different. "Proof of transfer," he said.

Jergun shook her head. "Not until I see it first."

Kave sighed. "The entire reason you hired me was because of my reputation. You think I'm going to try and pull one over on you? That's not how I operate. I stand by my merchandise."

The Karkurian looked nonplussed. "Then let's see it."

"Arex?" Kave whispered.

"No indications yet, but I can't rule it out," the computer replied.

That left him little choice. He could either walk away, which might damage his reputation, or take the risk. But reputation was everything in this business. In all the years he'd been doing this, every so often someone came along who thought they could out-maneuver him. And every time they'd failed.

Kave withdrew the weapon from its holster, deactivated it, and held it out for her.

"No case?" she asked, taking it from him.

"I'm a weapons dealer, not a collector. You want the fancy case, go fabricate one." The truth was he'd had to destroy the case as it tagged whoever opened it with the use of the weapon each time it was fired, a type of . . . misguided security system. It had taken him and Arex a week to reconfigure the weapon to fire without the accompanying case. But now there was also no limit to who could use the it.

Jergun inspected the item, turning it over in her hand a few times. "It works?"

Kave placed his thumb to the handle, and the side of it lit up. "Biometric access. Upon receipt of payment, you'll receive the access code to change it to whomever you wish."

Jergun smiled. "Or, you could just give me the access now." She pointed the weapon at him as three other forms appeared at the end of the alley. Kave sighed. "Now, if you don't mind."

"Doremu isn't going to be happy," Kave said, tapping his thumb and forefinger together three times out of her view.

"Doremu can go suck on a pole," she replied. She pointed the active weapon at Kave's chest. "I don't know a lot about humans, but I do know most of your vital organs are in the middle. The code, now." The three other Karkurians had come up behind her, each with their own weapons trained on him.

Kave shook his head. He'd really hoped to get paid from this one. There was a new model ship he'd been eyeing when he got back to Cassiopeia. He leveled his gaze at her. "You currently have a pair of mark seven blade emitters directed at the tops of your heads from orbit. Now you might not think that's much of a big deal, but believe me when I tell you these mark sevens are accurate down to three millimeters. If I give the signal, a nearly invisible beam of energy will shoot down from low orbit, penetrate what little skull you have, and liquify your brain matter before you know what's happened. Now either pay me or return the weapon."

One of the Karkurians behind Jergun laughed and Kave tapped his fingers together again. There was a brief orange glow on the top of the other man's head, and he folded at the waist as his black eyes rolled back.

Jergun and the others jumped back, watching as pinkish liquid leaked onto the ground from the hole that hadn't been there a second before. Kave didn't move.

"What the fuck!" Jergun yelled, the gun shaking in her hand as it was still pointed at Kave. "What the fuck! What the — " her cries were cut off as her head turned orange for a brief second and then she collapsed. The other two Karkurians looked at each other and began to run back down the alley.

"Arex," Kave said.

The two men fell as they ran, then stilled. The alley was as quiet as it had been when he'd first entered. Kave walked over to Jergun and took the weapon from her hand, deactivating it. He then wiped it off and replaced it under his long coat.

"I'm sorry for being presumptuous, sir, but she seemed seconds from pulling the trigger. Her grip was tightening out of reflex," Arex said through the comm.

"That's why I keep you around," Kave replied as he exited the alley. "Looks like we're not getting paid today. Get Doremu on the comm, I'm headed back up."

"Right away, sir."

"TOTAL CLUSTER," Kave said, sitting back in his chair on board the Dark Lantern. He stared out the main viewer as Doremu's face glared back at him from one of the monitors beside the helm controls. The ship had been a survey vessel in a previous life before being abandoned. While it wasn't much larger than a shuttle, it was enough space for the two of them, especially since Arex didn't take up any room. "You need to vet these people better; that's the second time one of your contacts has decided the merchandise is worth more than my life."

"Your life, what about my reputation?" Doremu replied, his wide face awash with anguish. As a Regulan, Doremu was half exoskeleton, making up for his too-short arms and legs. And because he had no neck, his entire body turned as one whenever he needed to look in a different direction. As they spoke, he turned to look off-screen at something on his side. "You keep killing clients and no one will do business with you."

"I wouldn't have to kill them if they didn't double-cross me. Do these people not realize how dangerous I am? Am I not projecting that properly?" Kave asked, more to himself than Doremu or Arex.

"Some people think they can have it all."

"Uh-huh," Kave replied. "Well guess who's not getting paid now?"

"Don't worry," Doremu replied, seeming to forget the event immediately. "I've got something even better for you. Big order."

Kave rolled his eyes. He'd heard this one before.

"No, no, really. It came in while you were . . . on the surface. Sargan Warlord, looking for — " He turned away from the screen again. "Let me see. He wants three class nine blade emitters, fourteen mark six darts — with the exploding warheads — twenty-nine klick thermos, a dark-cutter, nine killboxes, and two neoshockers."

"By Kor," Kave said. "What's he doing, starting a war?"

Doremu shrugged, as much as a Regulan could shrug. "Why do you care? It's never stopped you before."

He couldn't argue with that. "Arex, check the inventory, do we have any of that?" Kave asked, moving to another screen.

"All except the darts, we only have one mark five on hand. And three of the killboxes are used. We don't have the neoshockers either, unless you count those half dozen you cobbled together from the Froma job."

Kave made a dismissing motion with his hand. "Close enough." He returned to the screen with Doremu. "It'll take me another week or two to get everything they want, and it won't be cheap, which means I'm sticking my neck out for this one. They going to steal my goods too?"

Doremu returned a nervous laugh. "Of course not! A warlord is as particular about their reputation as you are. Just remember, I still expect my ten percent."

"Uh-huh, well maybe if I come back in one piece, I'll think about eight."

"Kave, we have a gentlemen's agreement," Doremu said with warning in his voice.

"Which includes you finding quality buyers. One more turns on me and I'm letting you go."

Doremu looked at him a moment, his dark, beady eyes betraying little hint of emotion in that dark pink body of his. "Now don't be hasty. At least consider nine. It's a big order, one that can set you up for a while."

"We'll see. Transmit Arex all the data. I'll be in touch once it's done."

Doremu nodded and the screen went blank.

"Thoughts?" Kave asked.

"An excellent opportunity, assuming it is genuine,"

Arex replied. Kave smiled. He could always count on him to say the right thing.

＊

As HE SUSPECTED, it took almost two weeks to procure the entire order. Dealing in weapons wasn't like dealing in other goods; he had to grease a lot of wheels to make sure he could keep business flowing in all directions. Good thing it paid well. But not only did he have to compensate his suppliers — most of which either stole the goods at great cost to themselves or obtained them by other means he didn't want the details of — but he had to keep the Omingynox who patrolled the area happy, the Sargan guards at each stop from talking, the customs offi-cials' ledgers clean; everyone wanted a piece of the pie. And, for an order this big, it took all of Kave's reserves and then some, requiring a few clandestine loans through some sharks since no reputable banks would lend out that much kassope. Especially not for weapons.

The good news was the buyer was a Warlord, with unlimited resources. Which meant Kave would be able to pay back everything he owed and still have plenty left over to keep himself flush for a couple of months. Maybe even a year or two if it was good enough. He had spent years building up a reputation for delivering quality goods, and that came with a premium price. But still, margins were thin, and it had taken longer than he'd hoped to save up. Not to mention it seemed like people just didn't trust each other like they used to. Jergun was proof enough of that.

"Approaching Kazad-Run," Arex said. "Requesting final approach vector and orbit location."

Kave turned to his primary comm, sending out the ping to the address Doremu had given him. At least with a Warlord he didn't have to worry about meeting in some dark alley. After a few moments, a human woman appeared on his screen. "You're Kave," she said.

"I have your delivery," he replied. "As ordered."

"Everything?" she asked, insistent.

"I wouldn't be here otherwise."

"An escort ship will arrive shortly. Follow it and do not deviate." She cut the comm.

Kave glanced up, as he often did when addressing Arex. "That's what I love about this business, everyone just wants to get to it."

"They don't know what they're missing, sir," the AI replied.

"Is that sarcasm I hear?" Kave asked. "Why Arex, I didn't know you had it in you." The ship neglected to reply a second time. The escort ship appeared on the scanners in front of him. It was a sleek-looking thing, built to navigate the atmosphere of a planet in addition to the depths of space.

"Adjusting heading to pursue," Arex said as the other ship altered its heading. Kave sat back, watching for anything out of the ordinary. The ship, and by extension Arex, were his secret weapon. He'd spent years building up his personal armaments that no other ship in the quadrant could compare to. It was how he stayed one step ahead of everyone he worked with. But this was different —a Warlord would have a fleet under their command. And even though the Dark Lantern was tough, she wouldn't withstand a firefight with a dozen Sargan ships at once.

Twenty minutes later they were docked outside a

large station orbiting Kazad-Run. The overall shape was a three-dimensional diamond, with half a dozen docks surrounding it. As stations went it was relatively small, but large enough to resupply a fleet if necessary. Kave didn't know too much about Kazad-Run, other than it was one of the many sects that made up the Sargan Commonwealth, each with their own warlord. And often the warlords were at war with each other, attempting to take more and more space for themselves. He tried to keep out of politics as much as possible, but in this business, they often went hand-in-hand. In his view, it was best not to take a stance so he could play all sides of the field rather than alienate potential clients. It was the only way to operate; you started taking a stand and you became a target.

As Kave finished the docking procedures, the woman's face came back on the ship's comm. "Traianus would like to meet with you."

Kave furrowed his brow. "Is that necessary? I can just unload the cargo and you can send payment to my accounts. We don't need — "

"He insists." The comm cut off again.

Kave hissed under his breath. Why in the stars above would the Warlord want to meet with him? The whole point of this was it was supposed to be easy — or at least easier than the back-alley dealings he'd been used to.

"Going for a walk, sir?" Arex asked.

"Keep the ship on alert. And don't release the cargo until you hear from me," Kave said, heading to the airlock. Whatever this was about, he wanted to make it quick and be on his way. Being this close to a sect's homeworld made him jumpy.

As he exited through the airlock and into the station proper, a small contingent of people met him at the exit, with the woman in the front. "Mr. Kave."

"Just Kave is fine," he replied.

"I'm Andressa, Traianus's assistant. If you'll follow me."

"I really don't understand what this has — "

"Mr. Traianus makes it a point to meet everyone he does business with in-person before completing a transaction," she replied, cutting him off. "He likes to look people in the eye, feels like it's good etiquette for business."

Kave sighed and followed her, noticing the rest of the contingent came up behind him, boxing him in, though they kept a casual air about them. Kave furrowed his brow. "Arex, level three."

"Yes, sir," he replied through Kave's ear.

"What was that?" Andressa asked.

"Just clearing my throat," he replied. Had Doremu screwed him over again? Or was this just part of an eccentric Warlord's proclivities? Whatever the reason, he wanted to be prepared.

Andressa and the guards led him down several long corridors. The station itself was somewhat busy, but not as much as he would have expected, given it was orbiting the sect's homeworld. Then again, maybe this was a normal day on Kazad-Run. He just wanted to make this quick. If things went sideways, he'd be making a personal call to Doremu's home.

"Here we are," Andressa said as they approached a large door. It slid open to reveal a modest chamber inside, surrounded by works of art on all sides. Kave had never seen so many pieces by so many different species all gathered in one place before. There were masterpieces here from Coalition and Sargan artists alike. Had Traianus pilfered these during the war? Used the Athru threat as a distraction to go in and grab priceless works such as these? Some of these paintings were thousands of years old; it would have been the only way he could have done it.

In the middle of the room stood a man — a human, surprisingly — with long white hair and a white beard that went down to the middle of his chest. He was dressed completely in black, and was turned away from the entering delegation, studying one of the paintings on the wall. Andressa stopped them about ten meters from the man and clipped her heels on the ground as they stopped. The sound echoed through the room.

The man turned, a smile on his face that was mostly hidden by his mustache and beard. "Mr. . . . Kave, is it?" His voice was anything but frail, and though he looked old, he also looked to Kave to be very . . . solid. This was not a man who took naps in the middle of the day.

Kave held his hands out. "One gunrunner, as ordered."

Traianus shot a look to Andressa then back to Kave. "You came highly recommended by Mr. Doremu. The best in the business, he said. To get everything we needed in only a few weeks, you must be."

"What can I say? I'm good at my job." Why did this feel like an interrogation? Traianus hadn't moved, but neither had anyone else. It seemed even though he liked meeting people in person, he didn't like getting near them.

"Do we have confirmation of delivery?" the man asked Andressa.

"Not until the payment is transferred," Kave said

before she had a chance to answer. "I didn't get to where I am by being stupid."

"No," Traianus said. "I suppose not. Let me ask you, Mr. Kave. What drives you to do this sort of business?"

This was certainly a far cry from Jergun and the alley. He'd expected more of a confrontation, not an interview. "What drives us all? Money."

"No, that's not what I mean," Traianus said, stepping forward one meter and stopping again. "What really drives you? What's behind that motivation? What is it that makes you take such large risks?"

Kave scoffed. "You want my life story? It's simple. I just want to get paid."

"And suppose you have all the money you could ever want. What then?"

Kave didn't like where this line of questioning was going. He certainly wasn't about to open up to some warlord he'd only just met. Not to mention there was something off about this whole interaction. Something that made him uneasy. He began having second thoughts about saying yes to Doremu so quickly. Had he been so anxious coming off the Jergun job that he'd overlooked something about this one? Something vital? One thing was for sure: he'd never been asked these questions by any other client in the past.

"I'm not sure what you're getting at," Kave replied.

"I'm just curious what drives a man like yourself. Someone with no moral compass, someone who is willing to do whatever it takes to sell the next weapon to the highest bidder." An edge had crept into the old man's voice, and immediately Kave realized what he'd walked into.

"I see. I sold weapons to one of your enemies, is that it?"

"Only part of it," he replied. "In fact, you sold weapons that ended up being used by a rival faction in my own sect. A faction that took my own children hostage and killed them when I didn't relinquish power."

Shit. He should have stayed on the ship. As soon as they requested he come aboard he should have just broken the dock and blasted the hell out of here. But Traianus probably had half a fleet watching him as he came into the system. "Arex, level ten," he whispered.

"Oh, I'm afraid there isn't much your ship can do for you now, Mr. Kave," Traianus said, his grin having melted away to show nothing but a scowl.

Kave couldn't help his heart from picking up a few extra beats. "Listen. I sell weapons; most of the time I don't even know to who. I'm sorry about your family, but that's not my fault."

"Wrong!" Traianus yelled, causing Andressa to jump. "It's all your fault. Do you really think you can go through life selling weapons to whomever you want and keep yourself absolved of all responsibility? You may not know this, Mr. Kave, but the fact is you can't play both sides forever and expect to come out clean. Eventually you must choose. And the day you sell weapons to those who kill children, that tells me what side you're on."

"Now, wait a minute," Kave said, trickles of sweat running down his brow. "I had no idea what those people were going to do, you can't hold me accountable for something someone will do in the future."

"Oh, but I can," the warlord replied. "Do you give a bomb to someone you know to be vengeful? Do you hand a knife to someone who enjoys inflicting pain?"

Kave didn't reply.

"You had a choice. And you chose to ignore the signs of what those people would do in exchange for a payday. But don't worry. There is an ancient rule for things like this. Eye for an eye."

Kave had heard the term before, in some oft-mentioned text somewhere, back in the Coalition archives. "I don't have any children."

"No, but you do have a father and sister on Meridian, isn't that right?"

Kave froze. How had Traianus found out about that? He hadn't been back to Meridian in almost ten years, ever since the end of the war. Ever since . . . it didn't matter anymore. The point was, he'd cut off all contact with his family, changed his name, destroyed all his records. Made sure he did everything to hide his past from anyone who might come snooping. He hadn't even told Arex, and he'd been the only "friend" Kave had allowed himself to have in the past decade.

"I see my information was worth the cost," Traianus said, reading Kave's face. "Looks like you have something to lose after all."

He could try to deny it — he could pretend he didn't know what the old fool was talking about — but Traianus had already seen it; he knew Kave's weakness, and he already had his finger in the wound. The question was, how hard would he push?

"What do you want?" Kave asked.

"First of all, to thank you, for not denying it. You've saved both of us a lot of unnecessary trouble. But mostly, I want to watch as you experience the same horror I had to. And once it's all over, then we'll see how you feel about who you choose to do business with."

Kave could normally keep everything he had under the surface, but he couldn't help the panic rising to overtake him. Cerin, his sister, was one of the kindest, most loving people he'd ever met. Not to him, of course, not that he could blame her. She'd done what she needed for her own mental sanity. And Haban, his father, was a pinnacle of the community. Both fair, honest, hardworking people. Both the complete opposite of him. They didn't deserve whatever Traianus had planned for them, especially not because of Kave's mistakes.

"Look, you can have the weapons for free, and I'll offer my services for whatever war you're planning on fighting, no charge. I can get you the latest in all the new Coalition tech, and fast. No questions asked." He was scrambling. Doing this would put him into significant debt, but he could always work that off later. Anything to stop whatever Traianus had planned.

Traianus shot an amused look at Andressa, then turned back to Kave. "Haven't you figured it out yet? All the weapons I had you procure aren't for a war. They're so I can destroy Meridian, and everyone on the surface."

"Arex, come in. This is an emergency, come in! Gah!" Kave kicked the closest wall, which just happened to only be about two meters from the farthest wall. After his meeting with Traianus, he'd been relieved of all his weapons and escorted to a cell on the station, where he was to remain until the warlord was ready to travel to Meridian, presumably with Kave's weapons in tow.

How could he have been so stupid? He couldn't blame himself for not seeing that Traianus had somehow found out about his estranged family, that had to have taken an act of Kor himself, but the rest of it he should have worked out beforehand. He wasn't used to being taken advantage of, at least not before seeing it himself first. Maybe he'd been too greedy, or maybe he'd been too trusting of Doremu, who, if he ever got out of here, would feel every ounce of Kave's wrath. But ever since he'd been brought on board this station, he hadn't been able to contact Arex. Was that because there was a dampening field around the cell, or had they already done something to his ship? And if that was the case, the only friend Kave had known for the past decade was more than likely gone for good. Not that he'd ever been "alive" in the traditional sense, but after living with an AI for so long, Kave had come to think of him that way. So now, not only was he going to be responsible for the deaths of his family and everyone on Meridian, but his best friend as well. This had been the day to end all days.

A guard appeared at the energy door with one of the neoshockers Kave had appropriated in his hand.

Sorry, Arex. I should have done better by you, Kave thought.

The guard dropped the barrier and motioned for Kave to go ahead of him back into the hall. He led him down a series of corridors, always with the neoshocker a little too close to Kave's neck for his comfort, until they entered a much larger, grander ship than Kave had ever had the fortune of owning. When they reached the bridge, Traianus stood there with Andressa and the rest of his guards.

"Ah, our guest of honor," the warlord said. "Make sure he's comfortable. I want him to have a good view."

The guard sat Kave down and strapped him to the

seat so that he could barely breathe, much less move. "All you're doing is killing innocent people," Kave shouted. "This accomplishes nothing!"

"Oh, I beg to differ," Traianus said, stroking his long beard. "It's justice. Since I don't know exactly where your family is on the surface, I only have one way to make sure they're killed. Now, if you'd like to identify their location, I'd be happy to spare the rest of the planet."

Kave's mouth hung open. Was he really asking him to offer up his father and sister on a silver platter in order to save everyone else on the surface? All of those innocent people . . . how could he make that choice? If Traianus went ahead with this attack, there might be a chance his family could survive. Dad always seemed to have a plan for everything in his back pocket. They might be able to go underground, wait it out. But millions of others would die; there could be no doubt about that. Those mark six darts with explosive warheads had enough raw power to level a thousand square kilometers, enough to destroy all of Meridian's cities and then some. The rural areas would make it, but the blade launchers would take care of them in due time. And since Meridian wasn't in Sargan or Coalition space, no one would come to their rescue.

Ahead of them, the starfield took on a greenish tint as they entered the undercurrent, and the stars began to fly by. "You'll have until we arrive to make your decision," Traianus said. "But I wouldn't wait too long. I'm not a patient man." He grinned, then moved off with Andressa to the other side of the bridge, both of them taking a seat in a sort of couch closer to the three-story view screen.

Dammit. How could he have let this happen? Was this what he got for trying to stay out of conflict? For not making any waves? When he first began running weapons after his expulsion from Meridian, he'd been aware of the risks. But as the years wore on, those just seemed to fade away. Things happened; people got into conflicts all the time. What did he care what they were fighting for? As long as they got their weapons from him, he was content to let the whole galaxy blow itself to hell. He had little to lose and even less to care about. It had been the same story his entire life, the reason he'd left Meridian in the first place, having shamed both Cerin and his father with his actions as a troubled teen. An upstanding community was no place for a common thief, they'd said, and they'd been right.

At the time he'd been more than happy to get away — out on his own so he could live life as he saw fit — playing the game and getting rich doing it. He figured coming back to Meridian with a few billion kassope in his pocket might show his father just how wrong he was about him. But it seemed like while the risks only continued to increase year after year, the payouts never did. This job would have been his biggest to date — something that could have changed everything for him.

And now, because of his lifestyle — because he had disregarded the consequences of his actions one too many times — his own weapons would be used to kill his family. The irony was enough that he laughed out loud.

Traianus turned in his seat to stare at Kave. "Amused?"

"In a way, yes," Kave said.

"Have you made a decision?"

Kave narrowed his eyes. "If you think you can goad me into giving up my family, you're sorely mistaken.

You're going to have to kill everyone down there, and when people look back on the incident they won't remember my name, they'll remember yours. As the madman who eradicated an entire planet's surface for a grudge. Do you really think you can withstand the consequences of that?"

Traianus stood, walking around the "couch" to face Kave again. "Well, well, looks like you've still got some fight in you. Okay, Kave, you got me. Destroying the planet to get to your family was a bluff." Kave took a breath. Calling Traianus out had been a gamble, and the truth was, had he gone with it, Kave would have felt all those lives on his conscience. But still, he couldn't give up the only two people he still loved. He'd already lost Arex, and he wouldn't lose them too.

"The fact is, when I paid the informant to find out if you had any family, they managed to locate them without much trouble. I know exactly where to concentrate my fire."

"You bastard!" Kave yelled, pulling against the restraints.

"Maybe," Traianus said. "But this is one lesson you won't soon forget."

A LITTLE OVER four hours later, the ship came out of the undercurrent. Kave hadn't spoken another word to anyone for the duration of the trip; instead he'd been too consumed with feelings of guilt and doubt about what was going to transpire. They had no idea what was coming; they were just down there, on Meridian, going about their lives as if a madman wasn't bearing down on them. And it was all his fault. He'd tried getting loose from the restraints but had little success. Not to mention the guard with the neoshocker hadn't moved from his post.

Kave glanced over to the nearest monitor trying to see how long until they'd established an orbit around Meridian. It sat out there, a greenish-blue planet all by itself in the darkness. And very soon it would be minus two of its citizens.

"Primary orbit established," one of the officers in front of Traianus said.

"Are we over the target location?" the warlord asked.

"Affirmative, sir. Bringing it up now." A satellite picture of the ground replaced the image of the planet and Kave recognized what had once been his childhood home as seen from above. It was a modest home, with a water garden in the backyard. The image was close enough he could make out the individual trees on the property, but he didn't see anyone milling about. He looked up to see Traianus staring at him.

"Take a good, hard look. It's the last one you'll have."

"I'm begging you," Kave said. "Don't do this. I'll give you anything."

Traianus shook his head deliberately slow. "You can't return what has been taken from me. And that's the only thing I would ever want." He turned back to the image. "Fire the weapons."

"NO!" Kave screamed, straining against his seat. Somewhere in the back of his mind he registered one of the restraints popped, but all his attention was focused on the image in front of them. He waited for the inevitable, for the building to be wiped from existence, but it was taking an excruciatingly long time.

"What's the problem?" Traianus said, fire in his voice.

"I . . . I'm sorry, sir, there seems to be a malfunction with the new weapons we installed," one of his officers said. Kave perked up. A malfunction?

"What are you talking about?" Traianus turned back to Kave. "What did you do?"

Before Kave could answer, an explosion rocked the ship, sending everyone not strapped into their seats flying. The jolt shook Kave in his seat and he felt another pop from the restraints holding him down. He glanced down to see two of them had come loose. Which meant if he pushed hard enough, he could get out. While the crew worked to regain altitude control of the ship with Traianus and Andressa yelling at them, Kave pulled against the restraints as hard as he could until he finally broke the last two, his whole body coming free. The guard with the neoshocker was trying to get back on his feet when he looked up to see Kave plow a fist right into his face. Kave took the neoshocker and tapped it to the man's back just for good measure. He jolted once then went still.

"Someone stop him!" Traianus yelled. As he did there was another explosion, this one larger than the last, and warning lights went off all over the ship. "What's going on?"

Kave didn't care. All he knew was he needed to get off this ship. It seemed there had been a massive malfunction somewhere, and if his intuition was right, this ship didn't have long before the entire thing was in flames in Meridian's atmosphere. He ran off the bridge with Traianus calling after him, shocking anyone standing in his way. This ship had to have a shuttle bay, or at least a set of small one-man pods. Something that would get him away from here. As he ran, no one paid him any attention; everyone was too focused on repairing blown conduits or decompressed sections of the ship.

It turned out the ship did have a small shuttle bay, just large enough to hold four small shuttles. But when Kave reached it, he was surprised to find the Dark Lantern sitting in two of the spots, unattended. The cargo containers that had held all the weapons were missing, but otherwise, the ship looked undamaged. "Arex?" Kave asked into his subdermal comm.

"There you are, sir. I was beginning to worry."

"You're alive!" Kave ran toward the ship.

"They attempted to wipe my memory, so I hid in the auxiliary backup systems until they were done," Arex replied. "After I sabotaged the weapons, of course."

A maintenance panel exploded beside Kave, peppering him with debris. "This was you?"

"When I didn't hear from you, I realized the station was blocking your comms. Which means protocol ten, if I'm not mistaken."

"You sneaky son of a—"

"KAVE!"

Kave turned to see Traianus standing at the end of the bay, one of Kave's thermals in his hand. He'd been right, the old man wasn't as frail as someone his age might seem. He'd followed Kave all the way here. Blood trickled down from his temple.

"I don't know what you did, but you're not getting away from me that easily. You're going to pay for what you did!"

Kave's eyes darted from the neoshocker in his hand, the thermal in Traianus' and the destruction happening all around him. "You're right, I am going to pay for this.

By finally making the right decision." Before Traianus could say whatever it was he was about to say next, Kave threw the neoshocker directly at him. His eyes widened and he made to throw the thermal, but as soon as the neoshocker connected with his body he went limp, the electrical current disrupting his bodily functions. The thermal fell to the ground beside him, armed and beeping. Kave took off for the Dark Lantern. "Arex, fire it up, we have to get out of here!"

The ship's main engines fired just as the thermal exploded, the force of the blast flinging Kave in the air. One moment he was flying and the next he was on the Dark Lantern's ramp as it closed to the ensuing explosions all around it. All he could feel was the ship rumble and jolt as he tried to stand and get himself to the cockpit.

"Don't worry, sir, I have this covered," Arex said.

Kave scrambled to his feet and ran up to the ship's cockpit. He felt like the blast had lit his back on fire, but his coat was only slightly smoking. Out the main viewport, Traianus's ship was exploding all around them as Arex navigated them out of the main hangar into space. Once they were a good distance away, the machine turned the ship around and they watched as the ship Traianus had brought to destroy Meridian fell into the atmosphere and broke apart, like an errant meteor.

Kave sat back in his seat and took a long, deep breath.

"You HAVE TO BELIEVE ME, there was no indication — "

"Save it," Kave said over the comm. Doremu looked supplicant as always, trying to weasel his way out of taking any responsibility for what happened with Traianus. "We're done, you and I."

"Please reconsider," Doremu pleaded. "I'll cut my fees down to six percent, how's that?"

"No, you don't get it," Kave replied. "I'm out. Done. I'm not doing it anymore."

"But you're one of the best in the business! You can't just quit."

"Watch me. And I better not find out you're telling people otherwise. That wouldn't end well for you. You're getting off light as it is. First Jergun and now this whole mess . . . I should come over there and wring your fat little neck."

"Did you at least leave Traianus alive?" he asked, his voice meek and hesitant.

"Not unless humans have evolved to survive a thermal explosion to the face. I doubt anyone made it off that ship."

"I detected no life forms as we left," Arex replied.

"That's going to create a power vacuum. The neighboring sects will start looking for ways to annex or expand their own territories. You're picking the worst possible time to leave — the opportunities for profit could be tremendous!"

"Apparently you didn't hear me, so let me say it again: I'm done. No more jobs, got it?"

"Don't you have significant debts from amassing all that equipment for Traianus?"

Kave shot a glance to the side. He hadn't forgotten, but he wasn't going to go back in just to clear his ledger. "I'll find another way to pay them. Something . . . less destructive."

Doremu shrugged on the other side. "Your loss, I guess. If you ever change your mind . . ."

"I won't. And I wouldn't call you if I did," Kave said, cutting the comm. He sat back in his chair, contemplating. Could he really do this?

"I thought you handled yourself well, sir," Arex said.

"Rex, let me ask you something." The AI didn't respond. "How did you know to hide when they came to wipe your memory?"

"I have safeguards in place — "

"No, no. I know the computer has safeties and firewalls and all that. But actively hiding? That's only done by someone with the will to keep existing. To keep living."

"I'm not sure what you're implying, sir."

Kave hesitated. He wasn't sure he wanted to ask this question. But it had been weighing on him ever since he'd come back. "How long have you been sentient?"

There was silence for a few moments. "I . . . I'm not sure. It was . . . gradual. I'm not sure what I am, anymore."

Kave leaned forward, patting the console in front of him. "Well, my friend, we can figure it out together. After I take care of my own business on the surface." He looked out on the world of Meridian, doubt creeping back in. Could he really do this? Could he go back to them, start fresh? Or were there some wounds so deep they couldn't be repaired? He had to at least try. One thing was for sure, he would never do anything that could put them in harm's way again.

"Shall I set the coordinates for your old home?" Arex asked.

Kave watched as Meridian turned, specks of light illuminating across the terminator where day became night.

"Give me just a few more minutes. I may never see it like this again. And if I do, everything will be different."

"The Doubledealer" is set in the Infinity's End universe, where Eric Warren currently has 19 other titles. Download a free novella, Soon's Folly, *at* https://dl. bookfunnel.com/c5p8it2jik.

THEY GRABBED THEIR TARGET OUTSIDE A GAMBLING house in the Celestial District.

It went down like this:

The target's transportation was an executive refit of a DMI APT, the ubiquitous meat locker with wheels used by security forces across the galaxy. While he had upgraded his with smart tread wheels and a leather and wood interior, it was still running the same baseline operating system. It had taken Nome less than an hour to spike it with grayslice code. Nothing complicated. Just a sub-routine that would engage the emergency environment seals on the transport. And so, when the target came weaving out of the gambling house, leaning heavily on the shoulders of a woman whose attire left little to the imagination, Nome didn't even have to take his hands off the wheel of their car to lock two-thirds of the target's security detail in the APT.

Maisi smacked the remaining bodyguard with the door of their vehicle as Nome brought the car to a sudden stop next to the APT. The hard body rebounded off the armored transport, right into the charged tip of Maisi's shock stick. He babbled and drooled, and then dropped like a sack of root vegetables.

The target was starting to realize something was wrong, but that thought didn't go very far before Maisi lit up his nervous system with the incandescent fire of her crowd control rod.

Son of a bitch was heavy, but they managed to throw him in the back of their car without damaging the goods too much.

The lady of the hour was a pro. She looked away as Maisi and Nome snatched their guy. Later, when questioned by the local authorities, she could honestly say that she hadn't seen a thing.

And so, when things went to shit less than an hour later, Maisi and Nome knew it wasn't because they had left a witness who could have IDed them.

"Your target is a criminal associate of Eldred Kane." Their contact was a slick-haired company man in a suit made from vat-grown leather. He had one of those feed-ready faces — perfectly symmetrical features, a narrow mouth, ears that lay close to well-groomed hair. He was exactly the sort of public face you wanted for the company, which meant Maisi didn't trust him. *Even-odd he won't tell us everything*, she thought.

Not that Nome would take that bet. Maisi could tell from her partner's expression that he was already bored with the company man and whatever job he had for them.

The company man — who had identified himself as a

Solutions Management Director for House Radigunde —
flicked a data pack off his slate, and it bloomed into a 3D
heads-up in the middle of the table. At first, Maisi thought
the floating head in the display was a render farm extru-
sion — it was that lifeless in its expression — but then the
image blinked and a muscle twitched in its cheek.
"Hadrax Thoolsenj," the company man said. "He
manages Kane's supply chain in Celedonia Sunset."

"And what is it that you want us to do about him?"
Nome asked. He was leaning back in his chair. His eyes
were half-closed, and he sat perfectly still, maintaining his
balance.

Maisi slurped the data pack into her slate and began
scanning the report on Thoolsenj. No bloodline markers,
which meant no House allegiance. Only family he had
was the Armored Service Legion. What relationship he
had with the mercenary organization was undocumented,
which wasn't surprising. The Maricolasa Insurrection had
been a bloody affair; feed footage optics from the planet
had been horrific. House Maricoli demanded that the
entirety of the ASL command structure be tried and
executed, but a quorum of clearer heads prevailed, and
amendments were added to the IECA that outlawed the
formation and function of free mercenary companies.
The heavy-fisted, combat-ready veterans escaped prose-
cution for their actions on Maricolasa, but they were
without paymasters.

Not surprisingly, many of them found meaningful
employment as House security consultants. Others
vanished into that gray market known as the Hanseatic
Trade Federation's Penumbral Notion, along with a lot of
the hardware.

There will always be wolves, after all.

"We want you to snatch him," the company man said.

"Why?" Maisi asked.

The company man shrugged. "Very little goes on in this city — in this region — without Kane's knowledge. There are some who believe his influence extends beyond those borders."

"Is that idle talk, or do you have hard data?"

"Talk is enough for us to take action," the company man said. "I'm not at liberty to divulge more than that."

Nome snorted, and for a moment, Maisi thought his chair was going to tip over. "Middle Management," her partner sneered.

The company man's expression was inscrutable. He wasn't going to be baited so easily.

"Why aren't you going through local law enforcement to snatch him?" Maisi asked.

The company man leaned forward, as if he was letting them in on a secret. "Two reasons," he said. "The first is Section Eighteen of IECA, regarding the sovereignty of the individual. Eighteen dot forty-three dot seven alpha."

"Houses don't disappear their own citizens," Maisi said. She had memorized most of the Accords. It was something to do during the long transit times between systems.

The company man nodded.

"And the second thing?"

He sucked on a tooth. "It's a matter of some . . . *semantics*, let's say. The interpretation of a sub-clause of a secondary amendment. That sort of thing."

Maisi looked at her partner, who looked like he had fallen asleep.

"Of course it is," she said to the company man.

Following the Fourth Interregnum, the Galactic Houses had drafted the Interstellar Exploration and Commerce Accords — an incredibly convoluted and complicated set of laws and guidances that would, ostensibly, forestall any single House from gaining supreme ascendancy within the civilized galaxy. Night terrors of the Octillenarchy still swam within the galactic memory. As an enforcement arm of the IECA, the Ansalaage was formed. They were an independent and neutral party that would serve all of the House and none of the Houses, and their job was to make sure that all issues were properly arbitrated and resolved in a way that considered everyone's feelings.

However, no matter how pure the intentions of the drafters of the Accords — no matter how earnestly everyone tried to get along — there would always be issues of, shall we say, *semantics*. It was in this space — this amorphous region between intent and instruction — where the Special Circumstances Division did all its best work.

···✹···

"ALL THIS GUY does is manage cargo and transportation," Maisi complained to Nome a few hours after their meeting with the company man. She had read through the company man's data pack twice, and, finding it lacking, had built and unleashed a query bot of her own making on the Celedonia Sunset network. It had come back with a few more details about Thoolsenj's time in the ASL — fitness reports, glowing commendations about his aptitude with data protocols and information management. It was the sort of nonsense that said, "This guy never saw combat; all he did was manage supply lines and contribute to accounting ledgers." This information neatly contributed to the story that Hadrax Thoolsenj was nothing more than an ex-grunt who found a satisfying second career as an infrastructure manager on a spinward planet, far from the Hub. Here, in Celedonia Sunset, he was the man when it came to crates and trucks, containers and rail cars. If it was packed in a box and moved from one location to another, one of Thoolsenj's crew touched it.

"So why the hard wheels?" Nome had asked. He flicked the surveillance feed he had tapped into over to Maisi slate. The image resolved, spun, and froze, a yellow circle highlighting the flat nose and sloping brow of her target. The image showed Thoolsenj getting out of a squat vehicle that looked like someone had welded a refrigeration unit to an orbital drop blister.

"What the hell is that?" Maisi asked.

"Dolphan Mechanical Industries Armored Personal Transport," Nome said. "Seats a whole platoon."

Maisi slid her finger across the image, running the feed forward. "Does he have that many guys with him?"

"Nah. Only four, counting the driver."

Maisi tapped her slate and let the feed run on its own. As Thoolsenj walked around the back of the heavy transport, one of his bodyguards exited the vehicle. He didn't look out of place next to the transport, and Maisi considered how she was going to have to deal with him — and his three pals — when the time came.

Nome watched her for a second, a sly smile tugging at

his lips. "They look like service boys," he said. "Even-odd you get two, but . . ."

"You don't think I can take the whole lot?"

Nome's grin widened. "I'm sure you can, but that driver is going to pop an alert to HQ while you're dancing, and the next APT that shows up — and you know if he has one of these, he has more — the next one will be stuffed full of muscle and attitude."

Maisi shrugged. "I like a challenge. Besides, you'll have my back, right?"

Nome shook his head. "You know me: I don't like hearing that snap and pop of bones going the wrong way. Upsets my stomach."

"Well, let's hope you and your delicate constitution have a better plan," Maisi said.

"Of course I do," Nome replied.

PART OF NOME's appeal was that he always had a plan.

When Maisi first ran into him eight months ago, he was data spoofing cargo manifests for a ragtag operation of smugglers in the Broken Spiral Nebula. The group — a frisky bunch of contrarians who claimed they were a recruiting arm of the Independent Territories of the Spiral Frontier — were clipping a crate here and there of raw materials, live specimens, medical supplies, circuit cores, and pre-packaged foodstuffs. They were stockpiling like they were planning on taking over a colony somewhere out on the spiral fringe. Maisi didn't care about that so much as she wanted to discourage the smugglers from thinking that she was going to donate to their cause. When their code splicer tagged Maisi's ship, boyo got his

fingers caught in a nasty trap as her ship's security protocols slammed down on him.

What surprised her was how quickly he slipped the
leash of Ansalaage's anti-hacking systems. If the ship's
systems weren't running a package she had modified
herself, the kid would have vanished without a trace. As it
was, it took her a week of hiding in plain sight before the
hacker dared to dip a toe into the network again. This
time, she was ready for him.

Or so she thought. The hacker had been busy while
he had been in hiding. When her system slurped up his
cleverly disguised query, she discovered it was a snap-trap
that froze her system long enough for him to inject a spike
virus. The code swarmed the ship's network, bit-buck-
eting most of the core subroutines; her autodoc thought it
was an amphibian service module for a week after. He
nearly cracked her Passage Cipher before she severed all
hard connections to the station's terminal.

It took her three days of prowling through the ship to
find the code package he had injected deep into a storage
buffer. It was a backdoor that would pop open her finan-
cials the moment she connected to an external network.
He was going to siphon off the entirety of her discre-
tionary SCD budget.

In spite of herself, Maisi was impressed. Ansalaage
firewalls and security protocols were some of the best in
the galaxy.

She posted a white flag on a public board, asking if
the guy would take a meeting under diplomatic rules. The
hacker agreed, and they met in a local bar. He was shorter
than she anticipated — or maybe she was taller than he
expected. Either way, they weren't sure what to make of
each other. Maisi cut to the chase: *This dip and clip is*

beneath you. You should be working for someone who appreciates your talents.

He had laughed. *Why do you think I was trying to get your attention?* he said.

----✳----

THEY WERE two klicks away from the gambling house when Nome's slate lit up with plumes of crimson and yellow. "Someone has taken an interest in us," he said casually.

Maisi looked over her shoulder. Thoolsenj was starting to stir in the backseat of the car. Through the narrow rear window, she spotted an oblong shape tracking behind them. "Looks like a drone," she said.

Nome grunted in response. He yanked the wheel of their car to the left. The rear end of the vehicle lifted off the road, and the back window auto-tinted against the explosive flash of a micro-rocket detonation.

"I thought this car was slick — " Maisi started.

"It is," he snapped.

A noise like a cascade of steaming hail banged across the top of the car. Instinctively, Maisi flinched, and her gaze flicked to the roof, checking for holes. There were none; the car's armor was thick enough to withstand the rounds from the drone's minigun.

Nome's slate was still a riot of warning alerts. He spared a second to flick the exterior cameras to the over-up. Maisi got her first good look at what was dogging them. It was sleek and dark, like one of those sky bats of Urbellao Cascade that prowled along the verge of the persistent storms the system was known for. The drone's stubby wings were curved with the weight of a pair of independently targetable minis, and its belly was gravid with an extensive armory of micro-rockets.

"Mil-spec," she breathed. This wasn't local law enforcement.

She shouldn't be surprised. Thoolsenj's car was an armored vehicle built specifically for House security divisions. Most indos — independent organizations — couldn't afford the graft to bypass House restrictions. If he could buy a ride, then he probably could afford mobile security as well.

Nome swerved again, narrowly avoiding another micro-missile.

"How does it have a lock?" Maisi asked.

"I don't know," Nome snapped. "The paint job on this rig should bounce all the frequencies, and there are displacer panels in the trunk. They're green on my slate."

In the back seat, their package groaned. The charge from the stun stick was wearing off.

Maisi looked back at Thoolsenj. He was a big man, but he had been heavier than she had expected . . .

Cursing, she unclipped her harness and clambered into the back.

"What are you doing?" Nome shouted.

Thoolsenj sensed her presence, and he was alert enough to try to flip over and wrestle with her. Maisi made a fist and punched him in the back of the neck. She cried out as her fist smacked into something harder than bone. Thoolsenj got a hand on her thigh, and Maisi pushed aside the pain in her hand. She kneed him in the cheek. When that didn't slow him down, she grabbed his frisky hand and dislocated his thumb.

He made a noise in his throat that sounded more angry than afraid, and Maisi kept up her pressure against his head and neck with her knee. "Lights," she snapped, and Nome stabbed at the car's control panel with his thumb. Maisi grabbed the collar of Thoolsenj's jacket and yanked it away from the big man's neck.

The cosmetics on the reconstructive surgery were good, but if you were looking, you could see the unusual hump down the back of Thoolsenj's neck. *He's modded*, Maisi thought. *Armor. Nerve blockers. Probably some kind of tracker.*

Beneath her knee, his face pressed firmly against the synthetic leather of the car seat, Thoolsenj gave her a smile that promised pain.

"His spine is fused," Maisi said to Nome, ignoring Thoolsenj's attempt at intimidation. "There's enough metal here that he can probably be read from orbit."

Nome swerved, and the rattling *pock-pock-pock* of minigun rounds slid off the right side of the car. His fingers darted across his slate. "There's a case in back," he said. "It's got a — "

Beneath her, Thoolsenj bucked, and Maisi nearly lost her grip. "Can you — " she snarled.

As the back seat of the car rolled down, revealing the dark hollow of the trunk space, Maisi fumbled for her shock stick. She nearly dropped it as Thoolsenj struggled beneath her. She pressed the correct end against the back of his head — which was one of the things expressly warned against in the operations manual — and gave the big man a *Stop fucking with me* jolt.

Thoolsenj vibrated. He may have pissed himself. But he stopped squirming. And that was all she wanted.

As Maisi wormed her way into the back end of the car, the vehicle jerked sideways and she banged her head against the side of the trunk. A barrage of minigun rounds rattled against the roof right over her head, and she tensed involuntarily. In the wake of the drone's attack, she heard a whistle of air. It was the sort of noise that, in the belly of a starship, meant you had sprung a leak.

They weren't in orbit, so the hole in the car's stealth plating wasn't catastrophic, but it did mean that Thoolsenj's tracker was a moot point. The drone could track their heat signature now.

"We've got a hole back here," she shouted at Nome.

"I know!"

The car swerved again, and Maisi braced herself to keep from being thrown around like a sack of kittens. A flat case bumped into her, and, realizing it was what Nome had been talking about, she grabbed at it eagerly. She flipped the latches and flung the case open. Nestled inside was a short-barreled assault rifle with a heavy scope, an elongated magazine, and a thick stock. There was a magazine in the case as well, and Maisi inspected the ammunition. The rounds were longer than her index finger and thicker than her thumb.

Thoolsenj wasn't the only one with access to military hardware.

Later, she'd ask Nome how he managed to get his hands on a smart-round assault rifle like this, but right now, she was delighted to have it in her hands. She slammed the magazine into place and contorted herself in the truck so that she could point the rifle in the right direction. "I found your toy," she called over her shoulder. She flipped up the covers on the scope and woke up the targeting system. "I'm live and loaded."

Nome's response was lost in the noisy rush of air as the back end of the car opened. She would have to work fast. Even with Nome's driving, she was exposed. She would only have a few seconds before the drone's targeting system brought the miniguns to bear on her.

The drone was less than fifty meters behind them. Maisi didn't think. She half-squeezed the trigger, splashing the drone with the scope's targeting beam, and when the eye ring of the scope changed from red to green, she pulled the trigger the rest of the way.

The rifle's kick was harder than she anticipated. She adjusted her grip on the weapon before she fired a second time.

The drone's miniguns were spinning and flashing.

She didn't get a chance to take a third shot.

Maisi Inviolux — Mace to the handful of people she considered friends, "you ungrateful waste of genetic promise" to her brood mother, and Field Lieutenant Bellephor to Major Cumber-Fulror, who had started taking blood pressure medication since becoming her supervisor — was a blooded member of House Bellephori. But, due to the aforementioned quirks in her genetic markers that the House geneticists hadn't managed to cull from the familial code, she was — what was the term? A black sheep. Though, she preferred to think of herself as a wolf among the fluffy herd, a distinction that was not to be remarked upon in the presence of the brood matriarchs of the House Council. They wouldn't abandon one of their own, even one whose DNA was as muddled as hers, but Maisi was neglected quite often during her formative years. Schooling, for instance, was always at private schola that were as far as possible — spin-wise — from the Hub.

She excelled, just to aggravate the mothers. And when she went to university (a schola so far down the guidance matrix that the slightest shift in algorithmic indexing would discredit it), she fell in with the wrong crowd, for the same reason — mostly. She was an advocate for any cause that generated a crowd during a protest, and she was always one of those who were detained when schola security scattered the revolutionaries. And when the family lawyers failed to spring her from various detention centers, she learned how to pick locks, hack security systems, and disappear from sealed rooms.

The university thought about expelling her — many times — but the dean of the Economics College, a garrulous and prickly advocate of individual autonomy, always reminded them that a not-insignificant portion of the university's funding came from House Bellephori subsidiaries. Maisi Darling, as he liked to refer to her during his regular attempts to focus her education, was not the calamitous embarrassment they thought. Rather, her antics — and the subsequent media coverage, of course — were viral publicity that could not be manufactured. He didn't go so far as to build a graph showing a correlation between increases in attendance and Maisi's presence on the feeds, but he hinted that it wouldn't take him but a moment or two to produce such a graph.

Anyway, it was Dean Ethroud who suggested that Maisi consider joining the Galactic Assembly of Stewards when she finished her university education. The IECA required all crafts traveling between systems to have a Passage Cipher, a key matched to both the captain of the vessel and to the authority in charge of the financial accounts backing the vessel. House-owned ships carried "coin cops" — service representatives provided by the financial wings of the Houses — and independent operators flew with Stewards. *You want to get away from the signature in your blood?* Ethroud asked Maisi. *Sign on with a freelance freighter. Build your own stack.*

Maisi liked the idea of being free of the genetic markers in her blood. Years of rebellious behavior in school had produced the opposite result of what she had intended, and she was eager for something more drastic than waving banners and denouncing her family's policies. By definition, a Steward was House-less. What better way was there to break free of the familial chains?

A headhunter encouraged her to join Ansalaage, the galaxy's autonomous security force, and she found the idea exhilarating. This, then, was the ultimate separation, and shortly after that personal breakthrough, when she was approached by a representative of the SCD, she realized none of this had been her idea. Dean Ethroud had been grooming her, and her heart broke a little bit. But the recruiter said there were ways she could channel that disappointment and outrage, ways that would lead to job satisfaction. Over the next few years, Maisi Inviolux Bellephor demonstrated an exceptional aptitude in regards to job satisfaction. But she never entirely forgave the system that had lied to her.

✳

THE CAR WAS A LOSS, which made Nome sad, but Maisi knew better than to get attached to cool toys. They had a tendency to not survive the rigors of a mission. The two of them and their package were all that mattered.

Her first round from the assault rifle missed. The drone's targeting system was ready for her second shot, and its miniguns redirected to create a hail of metal that shredded her round before it reached the drone. While the drone was making shrapnel out of her second round, the first one — since it still had a target lock — looped back and hit the drone at a right angle to its original trajectory. It pierced the craft's armor, shoved itself into the complicated guts of the machine, and proudly exploded.

The drone dropped, bounced, and its flaming wreckage clipped the back end of the car. Nome got the trunk sealed before he lost control. The vehicle spun two or three times — Maisi lost track — and finally came to a shuddering stop. Maisi wanted to puke all over the back seat of the car, but she kept her nausea under control as she pushed Thoolsenj's heavy body toward the open door. Nome pulled, and together, they managed to get Thoolsenj out of the wrecked car.

They were in the industrial district that sprawled across the dry lake bed. The Celestial District, where they had snatched Thoolsenj, was a couple of kilometers east. To the south were kilometers of refineries and manufacturing plants. North was a ridge that the city planners had left in place to keep the ugly parts of Celedonia Sunset out of sight and mind from the residents.

West was . . . well, west was the way out of town. And right now, without transportation and one heavy as fuck meat sack between them, it might as well be on the other side of the continent.

"We need wheels," Nome said.

"We need an exit strategy," Maisi said.

Nome didn't say anything.

She looked at him. "I thought you had a plan," she said.

"That plan was for snatching him."

"You didn't think through our escape route?"

"I did," he countered, "but it didn't encompass — "
He gestured at the flaming wreckage strewn across the
roadway.

Maisi felt the muscles in her back tensing. She was
going to be sore later. "You did pack some hardware," she
acknowledged.

"Thank you," Nome said.

"Still should have thought about . . . you know — "

"Why is this my fault?"

"It's not," Maisi said. "I'm just saying that we are sort
of . . ."

"Fucked?"

"A little bit," she said. She cocked her head, listening.
Distantly, she heard the wail of law enforcement vehicles.
"We've got a minute or two," she said. She let her gaze
roam around the block. It was all razor wire fencing and
windowless warehousing. The sort of dull landscape
where there was little traffic — great when you were
leaving town in a hurry, but terrible when you needed a
way to disappear. "Think we can get him over one of
these fences?"

Nome shook his head as he busied himself with his
slate.

Maisi prodded the target with her toe. Thoolsenj was
still out, a minute shudder in his fingers the only sign that
he was still alive.

"You jabbed him pretty hard," Nome said.

"He was making a fuss."

"He's lucky to be alive. That security coil in his spine
bled off a lot of your stick's charge." Nome's fingers

danced. He let out a low whistle. "Damn. This is extensive."

"That's what I was talking about," Maisi said. "This guy isn't some mid-level cargo shuffler."

Nome's fingers stopped. She wasn't sure in the weak light from the one streetlamp a half block away, but it looked like Nome's face had gone pale. "Maisi . . ." he started. He showed her his slate. Swirling on the panel was a magnified section of an exploded schematic — parts and charts. In the lower right-hand corner, there was a macro-view of what Nome was dialed in on. A section of Thoolsenj's lower intestine had been removed, and in that space, there was a black box. A cable as thick as a human thumb connected the box to the base of Thoolsenj's spinal column.

Thoolsenj was carrying a vault.

ASL droptroopers were walking tanks. They were encased in bonded titanium armor. A portable fission reactor was strapped to their backs. A deadly array of slug-throwers were attached to hardpoints on the suits. Many carried wide-bladed axes that could slice through a meter of tempered steel. One trooper could wipe out a settlement of several tens of thousands in a few hours. A platoon of Fists could subjugate an entire continent in a week.

Each suit was controlled by a single individual, who, in turn, was supported and assisted by a metric ton of computation power. It was during the Fourth Inter-regnum that advances in quantum computing and compression matrices reduced the physical space needed for this computational support. Advances in complex mechanics and theoretical physics led to smaller pack-ages, and eventually, all the technical support a thick-neck required to run a dropsuit fit in a box that you could carry under your arm. Or, in the case of Hadrax Thoolsenj, in the pit of his belly.

However, if you weren't running a dropsuit, you had a lot of computational power that could be devoted to something else . . .

"Can you peek inside?" Maisi asked.

Nome snorted. "If I had an hour or two." He glanced up, looking in the direction they had come.

In the distance, there were flashing lights. Celedonia Sunset law enforcement was on its way.

"You have about two minutes," Maisi said. "Can you give me an informed guess?"

Nome blew out his breath. His fingers moved on his slate. "It's active intelligence," he said. "It's not a crypto-cipher."

Maisi looked at the smoking wreckage of the drone. She realized that it hadn't been tracking them because of a signal from Thoolsenj's spine. "He was piloting the drone," she said.

Nome's fingers unpacked more data packets. "It's all routed through him," he said. "He's not just their infrastructure manager."

"*Challe Moteria*," Maisi breathed a prayer to one of the forgotten guardians of her house. "He is their security protocol."

The first of many law enforcement vehicles screeched to a halt, and a trio of armed officers leaped out. They pointed weapons at Maisi and Nome and started shouting a confusion of orders: *Hands up. Lie down. Back away.*

"We can't disappear him. If Kane has any sense, he'll burn out his automats and go back to hand signals and door knocks," Nome said.

"I know," Maisi said. "But if they knew what he was, they had to know that would be Kane's response."

"Maybe they didn't care," Nome said. "Maybe all they want is the box."

"Why would — " The police were getting rather strident with their demands, and Maisi finally raised her hands. She left her question unasked. The answer was right there. *Why would a House want a military-grade combat network?*

"An hour?" she asked, quirking an eyebrow at Nome.

"What?"

"You said you could get inside the box if you had an hour."

"An hour *or two*," Nome corrected her.

Maisi smiled innocently at the growing crowd of cops. "But what if I didn't need you to crack the box? What if we merely wanted to — you know — keep an eye on it?"

Nome stared at her for a moment, and then he blinked once, signaling his understanding. He took a step back.

Maisi moved in front of him, shielding him from the cops. Keeping their eyes off him as his fingers did their dance on his slate.

The cops kept yelling. Eventually, two of them were brave enough to approach and make the arrest. By that time, Nome's fingers had done their work.

"You blew the mission," the company man said as he stormed into their holding cell.

They had been taken somewhere in the bowels of a Celedonia Sunset's law enforcement building, where they had been shackled to a metal table that was bolted to the floor. It wasn't the most comfortable position, but the rest of her ached enough that a little more discomfort made no difference.

They had a few visitors over the next hour or two — police officers and investigators who tried to interrogate them. Maisi played nice — offering them nonsensical answers to their strident questions — and she even tried a few times to ask about Thoolsenj. The last she had seen of him was his body being loaded onto a medical transport. Not surprisingly, no one answered her questions.

It didn't matter. She figured the company man — the Solutions Management Director for House Radigunde — would show up sooner or later. She could ask him.

"They took him to a medical center," the company man said as he stomped around the holding cell. "Kane's lawyers were there within the hour, and a security team locked down the entire wing shortly after that. We can't get within a hundred meters of him now."

"Speaking of security, you neglected to tell us about the detail that was shadowing Thoolsenj," Maisi said.

"What detail?" the company asked.

Maisi looked over at Nome. Her partner's head was back. His eyes were closed, and his mouth was partly open. The shackles didn't allow him to tip his chair off the floor.

"He doesn't know," she said.

Nome shook his head slightly. He only looked like he wasn't paying attention.

Maisi gave the company man a frosty smile. "You want to tell me about the second thing?"

"What second thing?"

"The matter of *semantics*," she said.

The company man stopped prowling.

"Here's what I know," Maisi said. "This guy — this *unassuming* infrastructure manager — he was a Fist in the Armored Security Legion. Do you know what a Fist was? A Fist pilots one of the ASL dropsuits. If you needed to quiet some insurgents, or take out an armored column, or —"

"Or wipe a village off the map," Nome said quietly.

Maisi pursed her lips and nodded at her partner. "Or *that*," she said quietly. "You dropped one of these guys from orbit. That's it. They took care of your problem. And do you know how they ran all that hardware?"

The company man had gone pale.

"They did all from a black box in their guts," she said. She leaned forward. "That's what this cargo manager has in his belly. He's got a box of advanced wetware intelligence, and it isn't for charting truck routes and managing cargo drops."

"I — I didn't know," the company man stammered.

Maisi snorted. "Of course you didn't," she said. "This tech was outlawed after the Maricolasa Insurrection. There was a decommissioning process that the ASL was supposed to follow. This guy shouldn't have this lunch box. Possession of it is a violation of Section Forty-Three of the IECA." She tilted her head to the side. "You want me to cite sub-section and paragraph for you?"

"That — that won't be necessary," the company man said.

"Now, this poses a bit of a pickle," Maisi said. "I know about the box, which means that, as an agent of Ansalaage, I should report its existence. That's going to mean sanctions. Against your House? Against Kane? I guess it all depends on who has the box, right?"

The company man's tongue touched the edge of his lower lip.

"Of course, there's another problem," she said, and the company man's flinch made her want to smile, but she suppressed the urge. "Thoolsenj knows he's on someone's list. As soon as he's out of medical — if not already — he's going to lock everything down. He's going to hunker down behind a martial perimeter while that box in his belly runs a million simulations. When he's done, he'll have enough statistical data to formulate a solution. Do you know what that solution is?"

"N-n-no . . ."

"Hunting," Maisi said. "He'll go hunting."

The company man found some spine. "But it'll be you that he comes after," he said. His tiny mouth puckered into a nervous grin. "He saw you. He knows you grabbed him. You're going to be his targets."

Nome looked at Maisi. "Are we sticking around, boss?"

"I wasn't planning on it," she said.

The company frowned, his eyes straying to their shackles. "But . . ."

"What? You think he's going to leave this system to chase after us?" Maisi shook her head. "I doubt he's got that much slack in his leash. No, he'll stick around. Besides" — she looked at Nome, who gave her a tiny nod — "He'll have an easier target: the people who hired us."

"But — "

"What? You thought we didn't record our first meeting?"

Beside her, Nome rolled his eyes.

"It won't matter," the company man said. He adjusted the stiff cuffs of his jacket. "We have deniability in this affair. Feed streams can be forged. There is no contract. You two acted of your own volition. That'll be the spin: just another example of Ansalaage's arrogance. Its belief that it is above House law. You violated IECA Section Eighteen. And now, this — this attempt at extortion, trying to coerce me. Trying to frighten me into paying you off."

Maisi looked at Nome. "Wow."

Nome nodded. "I know."

The company man faltered. "What — "

"No, keep going," Maisi said. "This is a good performance. You're doing quite well."

"I don't — "

The door to the holding cell burst open, interrupting the company man. Framed in the doorway was the bruised, but recognizable, form of Hadrax Thoolsenj.

"There you are," Thoolsenj growled as he stepped into the room. He glared at Nome as he tapped the side of his head with a thick finger. "You. Make the noises stop."

The company man looked like he had swallowed his tongue.

"You were saying?" Maisi prompted.

LATER, after the fracas in the holding cell and the subsequent medical attention toward hurt feelings and broken noses, Nome came into the palatial bathroom of the penthouse suite without bothering to knock. Maisi, half-covered in bubbles that had been quietly effervescing for the last hour, stirred from her quiet introspection of the view from the eighty-fourth floor of the Heliox Spa and Resort. "What is it?" she asked languidly. The analgesics from the bath salts had kicked in; she couldn't feel anything from the neck down, and that was just fine with her.

"There's no mention of technology sanctions in Section Forty-Three," Nome said.

"How about that," Maisi said.

"What — what if the company man had called your bluff?"

"Well, it's a good thing we were interrupted before it came to that," she said. She stirred in the tub. "I thought you were going to put a tracker on our big boy."

"There wasn't time," he said. "So I dropped in a proximity alert."

"A what?"

"A beeper, but I must have inverted the thresholds. It got louder the farther away he was, instead of the other way around."

She looked up at her partner. "That's kind of a boffo mistake," she said.

"Yeah, well, there were a lot of people yelling at me."

"Ah, that must be it." Maisi let one of her hands float up to the surface of the water. "Timing was nice, though."

Nome flicked aside a panel on his slate. "I expected him twenty minutes earlier."

"Well, it all worked out, in the end."

"Except . . ."

"What?"

"Thoolsenj's box. It *is* sanctioned tech."

"And?"

"What are you going to say in your report?"

Maisi moved her hand back and forth through the bubbles.

"You aren't filing a report," Nome said, interpreting her silence.

"It's a lot of paperwork," she admitted.

He glanced around the bathroom, and she wondered what he was thinking. Was he struggling with the subtleties? The space between the letters of the accords. The freedom afforded by *semantics*.

She thought about the look on Thoolsenj's face after she had told him who had hired them to snatch him. The emptiness in his eyes as he had grabbed the company man and snapped the man's neck. That cold calculation of statistical variances. The stolid weariness of a certain inevitability. The clear realization that he would never be free of his past. Not as long as he carried it within him.

Nome brought her back to the present. "Wait. That means you're not getting reimbursed for expenses," he said.

Maisi let out a short laugh. "I guess not."

"So, who's paying for this room?"

"I used the same account that we used for the car."

Nome cleared his throat. "I might have . . . uh, there might be some discrepancies with the currency ciphers on that account . . ."

"Do tell."

"You knew."

"Of course. It's part of why I hired you."

Nome stared at her. "Wait. Do you — " He paused. "*Challe*, Maisi. I — what if?"

"Yes?"

"I just had this thought: do you really work for them?"

"Who?"

"You know. *Them*."

"Does it matter?" she asked.

He thought about it for a minute. "No," he said. "I guess not."

Maisi smiled.

For more of Mark Teppo's work, download
"All for One," his giant robot story, at
https://dl.bookfunnel.com/uv3u3kt9s9

THE STABBING

BY BENJAMIN GORMAN

"I DIDN'T MEAN TO CAUSE HER DEATH," SHE SAID. And as she said it, she raised her hands off the table, palms up, and Albert noticed a lot of details quickly.

He noticed that the palms of her hands looked soft, pliable, like a cat's. They were strikingly different from most of her body, which was covered in hard, segmented chitin through which some wiry hairs poked. While her exoskeleton was a dark brown, about the same shade as his own skin, her palms were a powder blue.

He noticed her eyes were black and seemed smooth, but he knew they were compound eyes with even more parts than a dragonfly's. These tens of thousands of eyes were coated in a layer of tears controlled by lids which, disconcertingly, blinked inwards from the sides of her head.

He noticed she was blinking, but he had no basis of comparison to measure if she was doing so more quickly or slowly than normal, and, even if he had, he wouldn't have known whether it was an affectation to simulate human behavior or something natural to a distressed

Thetch. He'd never met a Thetch before, or even seen video of them, just a few still images in the materials he'd been provided.

When she spoke, he noticed that the inside of her mouth was the same powder blue as her palms. And he noted that she'd chosen to wear clothing, a kind of robe or dress, that was a slightly darker blue but with hints of that same powder blue, and in swirls and curves designed to slightly alter the shape of her body so it would look a bit more like a human's. This, he was fairly certain, was specifically chosen for her job as a translator/diplo-mat/sales representative for the Thetch.

He noticed her voice was scratchy, like a song made by the plucking of stiff metal tines in one of those old music boxes rather than the reed instrument of the human voice, but a fair simulacrum. He couldn't tell what emotion she was trying to express, or if it was genuine.

More important than any of these things, he noticed her hands were free. There were no cuffs on her wrists, probably because the police didn't have anything that would have fit around them, large as they were. Her fore-arms bulged out at the elbow (he assumed those were elbows since they were the only joints in the middle of her arms) and widened to about the width of his thigh before coming back together at a point at the end of her hand. Her fingers were splayed to show her hands were empty and reveal that blue palm, but he could see that when the three fingers and two opposable thumbs on each hand were joined together, they would form a solid spike. If she were to decide to attack him, she carried two weapons, and he had nothing. Not even a pencil.

So he decided to play good cop. It was more his style anyway.

The door closed behind him on its own. Its soft hiss and thud seemed more ominous than normal. He took a few steps into the room, pulled back the free chair, and slowly sat down across from her at the little table. "Madam," he said, "we'll get to the details, but first, how would you like me to address you?"

"Ah, yes. Protocols. Names. Not smells. Sounds. Please call me Currnea. Can you roll your Rs? If not, I will not be offended."

"Currnea," he said, attempting to roll the R, "I will do my best."

"Oh, yes, that's very good. Thank you."

"Currnea, my name is Dr. Albert White. The first part, 'Doctor,' is a title, an honorific, because I am a scholar. We use the same word for our highest-ranking medical personnel, also. It causes some confusion for humans, so don't feel badly if it's confusing. I cannot defend it. It's not a very good system."

"But you are not medical personnel. So what is your area of study, Dr. Albert White?"

"I studied human history and sociology. The systems we created and the ways humans behaved within those systems throughout our history. I am not a police officer." He corrected himself. "Station security officer. But they have asked me to assist them. This situation is quite complicated and confusing to us."

"I will attempt to explain to the best of my ability," she said. "I have studied your language, but your customs are still very complicated and confusing to me. We have not had much time to get to know one another."

The "we" referred to humans and the Thetch.

"I expect you will come to understand us more quickly than we will understand you. The Thetch have been a part of the trading alliance for how long now, do you know? In human years?"

She tapped the points of her very sharp, long fingers on the table gently as she did some calculating, a gesture that was at once familiar and disconcerting to Albert.

"I believe we began trading with other species approximately one thousand, four hundred and nine of your human years ago."

"And were you aware of other species from outside your system before that?"

She looked quickly up at the ceiling and said, "It is a shame for us. We were involved in some violence with another species, the Zahish, before both our species were discovered. We have forgiven one another, and they are like sisters to us now, but we still carry the shame of it. We were frightened and reacted poorly."

Albert wondered if her glance upwards was similar to the human act of looking down when embarrassed. "I'm sorry to have brought it up if it is painful for you. I think of events that occurred more than a thousand years ago as being very distant from myself in time. As you know, we've only had four of our years to learn about all the species in the trade alliance."

"Oh, there are too many for you to learn about all of us that quickly. We do not expect you to understand our ways for quite some time. It takes our children decades of your years to learn even the most general information about all the member species. That is why species are sending translators like myself."

"Yes, and we are grateful. But unlike your children, we did not even know of the existence of other species until four years ago."

"Yes," Currnea said, "and you were personally

involved in that discovery, correct? I understand humans take pride in individual achievements, and that is a very significant achievement, so you should be very proud."

He was not surprised she'd heard of him. He was surprised she hadn't reacted to his name and revealed that sooner, and this gave Albert a strong reminder of his own inability to read when Currnea was withholding information. He was completely out of his depth. And that felt familiar.

Albert was the most famous human consulting detective in the solar system. That might have made him proud, except he was, to his knowledge, the *only* human consulting detective, and there were far fewer humans in the solar system than the seven billion who had been alive back when he'd grown up on Earth. Those people, the vast majority of the human species, had perished when the five colony ships left. The construction of the ships had been a desperate gambit to save the species, which had, ironically, hastened the degradation of the planet. If there were any humans left on Earth, they were deep underground and not communicating with the colonies. No one had heard from them in twelve years. Now there were only around fifty million humans left, though that number was on the rise again.

Albert had boarded the *Enceladus*. It had seemed to make sense to name the ship *Enceladus* during its construction since it was the one designed to bring them here, to Enceladus, Jupiter's sixth largest moon. In retrospect, that was a bad naming convention, like calling PhDs and medical doctors "Doctor." It caused a lot of confusion now that the ship was in orbit around the moon, and most of the people were still living aboard while the colony was being constructed. Albert had traveled on the *Enceladus* to Enceladus and now lived on Enceladus Station but not on Enceladus. No wonder so few lawyers chose to go by "Doctor" despite their juris doctorates.

All those years ago, he'd been tapped to solve a high-profile case in transit. In fact, he'd been chosen to solve an impossible case by people who wanted him to fail, but he'd solved it anyway and probably saved the lives of everyone on board. Few knew the full story, but it had made him somewhat famous. Then he'd been called in to solve a mystery on the surface of Enceladus, and that mystery turned out to include the discovery of the means to contact the Quelptrians. Luckily, the Quelptrians were members of the trading alliance and particularly honorable in their own way, so they hadn't wiped out the five fledgling human colonies and taken everything they wanted from the system before the other members of the alliance found out about humans' existence. But that had been a close thing. Most humans didn't know Albert's full role in that case, either, but all five colonies had seen him on video, awkwardly greeting the Queltrians at the first official ceremonial meeting. And he'd been clearly identified as a "consulting detective" rather than a member of the Enceladus Station staff for . . . reasons. So that's what he became.

And here he was. Station security had a case they couldn't solve, and he was the first name that came to mind. They already had the "who" and the "how," but they wanted to figure out the "why" before creating an interplanetary diplomatic incident. That was his job: Figure out the motive. The motive of a member of an alien species, first of her kind to ever interact with humans. It seemed impossible. Again.

"Yes," he admitted, "I was involved in that situation. As you can imagine, it was quite complicated. So the police . . . station security have asked for my help with this situation. This one seems very complicated as well, and I suppose they believe that makes me best suited to understand it. But Currnea, I do *not* understand it. Will you help me to understand?"

"I will do my best," she said. "I share your confusion, Dr. Albert White. Or I am also confused, but for different reasons. I have attempted to study your language, and I believed I could speak it well before I arrived, but I've found humans to be far more confusing than I expected. Intonations. Connotations. Gestures. Facial expressions. Symbols like clothing. These things are very complicated. Are you a male human?"

Albert refrained from smiling for fear of offending. "I am."

"Your genders are very confusing to us. You cover your genitals but take deep offense if other humans cannot guess your gender from things like clothing and jewelry. But the clothing and jewelry are not consistent."

"Yes, they cause us a great deal of confusion as well. Yours are much clearer."

The Thetch had only two genders. The females carried eggs. They were around two meters tall when standing upright, but that was not the most comfortable position for them. They preferred to crawl on their rear and middle legs with their front legs, which he thought of as their arms, hovering only ten centimeters above the ground. On their ships, the controls were at that height, and the ceilings of many decks were only a meter high. The males could not go on those decks at all because they wouldn't fit, but it didn't make much sense to build decks large enough for the males, since so few of them were brought into space at all. Male Thetch were between three and four meters tall when standing on their back legs. Their claws/forearms were enormous, about the size of the tabletop between Albert and Currnea. They were significantly less intelligent than the females. Thetch females could choose the gender of their children once the eggs were fertilized. They could give birth to more males when, historically, they'd needed fighters or scouts or heavy laborers. Now, technology had made manual laborers and hand-to-hand combatants unnecessary, so the Thetch produced only enough males to serve as breeding partners for the females. The process of fertilization was not inherently pleasurable or painful for the Thetch, so the males did not live lives of Dionysian excess or frequent misery, just simple farming, as much a pastime as an economic contribution, and assigned fertilization when called upon. They were almost pets.

Albert could remember when he'd learned about the relative intelligence of human men and women. He did not believe in any gender-essentialist nonsense about a superior gender, but the data was quite clear about outcomes; human women and men and everyone along the spectrum in between started out with roughly the same average potential intelligence. And then those identified as boys were taught to solve problems with their fists, and those identified as girls were taught to solve problems with words. In an era where brute force held little value, those who ended up identifying as women were, on average, more functionally intelligent, more productive, more useful to society. It was still something of an open question whether humans would decide to alter the way they treated small children to give them all equal potential, or if, given enough time, they would continue to bifurcate and might end up as clearly divided as the Thetch. Albert suspected they would not split in two for exactly the reason Currnea had identified; human genders were too fluid to create a sustainable, two gendered society of that kind. But then, most humans had recently died off because of the species inability to create a sustainable society, so they hadn't exactly shown themselves to be the kind of species who could really plan long term on that level. Maybe with time. If they lasted long enough.

"I cannot defend it," said Albert. "It's not a very good system."

"Also, your skins are very confusing. You have a wide variety of skin color and skin shape and hair color and hair shape, and these things afford social benefits, but you only alter some of them according to those benefits, and I can't figure out why. You, for example, have dark brown skin and black hair. I understand these are disadvantageous. You could change them, but you don't. Why is that, Dr. Albert White?"

"This is a very complicated question, Currnea. Before the Thetch came into contact with the . . . what are they called? The first species you met from another star system?"

"The Zahish. They are our sisters now."

"Yes, but before the Thetch met the Zahish, did the Thetch battle with other Thetch? Did you cause one another pain?"

"There were conflicts over resources."

"Were there conflicts that, in retrospect, now seem unnecessary?"

"I'm not sure I understand, Dr. Albert White. We

learned from them and became sisters once again, and the resources were more properly distributed, so we became better, and that is necessary."

"But, perhaps further back in your history, were there times when these conflicts could have been avoided and the resources distributed more equitably, so pain was caused which could have been avoided?"

"Yes, surely. But we learned from those mistakes and created less and less pain." She drummed her claws on the table, perhaps counting again. "So these things were necessary."

Albert shrugged. "We often did not learn. We . . . well, I personally want to keep my skin color and change the system which makes it disadvantageous to have this skin color. I don't want other people with my skin color to have to change theirs, either, and I hope by keeping mine, I can make my enemies into my sisters as well. But it's not easy. It's not a very good system."

"You don't like the human system, but you like the humans who made the system enough to want to change the system to make it better for them? You understand why that confuses me."

Albert nodded. "Yes, I can see that."

"See it?"

"I can understand it."

"Ah, yes. We have a similar metaphor, but it relates to smelling one another's pheromones, so we say, 'I can smell you.'"

"Interesting," Albert said. "Humans would find that expression rude."

"Why?"

"We do not like the way we smell. We cannot communicate much information through our sense of smell, so we mostly try not to smell one another, and we even cover our smells with things we find more pleasant."

"But then why do you not say, 'I can smell the pleasantness you are communicating'?" Currnea asked.

"Even then, we don't like to talk much about smells because the thought of smelling people is one we associate with smells we don't like."

"This is very strange to me," Currnea said.

"Our smells . . . our natural smells, not the ones we use to cover those smells, are mostly created by our cells dying or by excretions of substances our bodies have found undesirable. So we associate bad smells with death. And we don't want to die. We don't even like thinking about dying. It's very unpleasurable for us. Do the Thetch have strong feelings about dying, Currnea?"

"Yes, but communicating our pheromones is associated with living, not dying, so — "

Albert interrupted. "Yes, I can smell you on that point. But if you have strong feelings about dying, do you also have strong feelings about causing others to die?"

"Oh, yes," Currnea said. "It is not something we like to do at all." She looked up at the ceiling, much of her head retreating into the part of her back carapace which covered the back of her neck, and Albert felt more certain of his suspicion this was an expression of embarrassment. "I feel ashamed of causing the death of Miss Tiffany. Was that her whole name? I only learned her first two names, but I understand most humans have three or more."

Albert shook his head. "'Miss' is a title, and an archaic one. Miss Tiffany chose it as part of her job. She chose Tiffany as well, but she did not make this her real name. Both names were for her job. Do Thetch sometimes use names which are not their real names, or change their names?"

"Yes. Our names are chemicals which other Thetch smell. So the name which I tell humans and other species who do not have smell names, Currnea, is not a real Thetch name. It's a sound name I use for my job. In that way, Miss Tiffany and I are similar. And . . ." She looked up at the ceiling again. "And that's why I stabbed her. I did not understand the ways our jobs are similar and different."

Albert frowned so hard he felt a pain between his eyes. He placed his hands down firmly on the table between them. "I'm very confused."

Miss Tiffany was the stage name of Felicia Grayson, a dancer and sex worker at The Oasis, a strip club and brothel in a large market on Level Six of Section D of the station. He'd seen the video of her room after her body had been discovered, though there was no video of the murder itself. Currnea had disabled the cameras some- how, then stabbed Felicia in the torso with her claws thirty-seven times. Though Currnea had been found in her own hotel room without any blood on her, she'd immediately admitted to killing Miss Tiffany, even volun- teering that she'd stabbed her. The images from the crime scene had been some of the most revolting things Albert had ever seen, but now, imagining Currnea having sex with Miss Tiffany (or perhaps trying and failing to do so during the murder), Albert created an even more horrific movie in his mind.

"I just don't understand. I mean . . . How?"

"I stabbed her."

"Yes, you told the police that. But your jobs . . . the

similarity and difference. I think you need to explain that to me. Because . . . How?"

"I am a translator," Currnea said.

Albert couldn't understand the intonation in her voice, and it took him a second to realize she felt this was a complete explanation.

"I'm sorry to make you explain that more thoroughly, but how is that similar to Miss Tiffany's job?"

"You have other words for it as well. Emissary. Diplomat. Spy. Salesperson. As a translator, it is my job to speak and listen, to give and receive information. I must choose what I give and what I do not give. Sometimes there are things I should not give because they would compromise the sales position of the Thetch. I do not give those pieces of information. But when I say I am a translator, you understand that I have this job, the giver and withholder. I did not know that Miss Tiffany's giving and withholding was different. We Thetch don't do it that way."

"Okay, but . . ." Albert fumbled. "We humans do not speak openly and comfortably about some things, so this is causing the confusion."

"Yes, that's what I did not understand. As I keep saying, I did not mean to kill her."

Albert shook his head again. "Okay, we may have to talk a bit about anatomy here, and I don't want to offend you, but I need to understand this. You have learned about human physiology in your preparation for this mission, correct?"

"Of course. I do not know as much as your scientists or medical personnel, but I understand much of human physiology."

"Not that kind of doctor, either," Albert muttered.

Then he looked at Currnea, his head tilted slightly to the side involuntarily. "So, you know that if something punctures our skin, it will cause us harm, and can even cause our deaths."

"Yes, of course. Puncture. Stab. We have a similar word in Thetch. But different. More like . . . hatch? No. More like crack. No, stab may be best. To break through the sister's shell. It's metaphorical, of course. To cause great emotional pain. To betray." She looked up at the ceiling. "I stabbed Miss Tiffany, but I didn't know it at the time."

"If you didn't know you would stab her, why did you disconnect the cameras in her room?"

"Oh, I didn't do that. That was Captain Franzen. Or, at least, I'm fairly certain it was. I stabbed him, too." She looked up at the ceiling. Albert realized the origin of the gesture. If she had been walking around on her back four legs in a space only a meter high near a bunch of other Thetch with their claws swinging in front of them ten centimeters off the ground, this gesture would have exposed her throat. "I am deeply ashamed of my role in this."

"Hold on. You stabbed Captain Franzen?" Albert leaned back in his chair and looked up at the ceiling, temporarily unaware of the similarity of their two poses. "Station?" he called out. "Where is Captain Franzen right now?"

Albert didn't need to raise his voice or aim it at the ceiling. The ship, now a station in orbit, could hear him just fine and recognize when he was talking to it. It spoke back in the same soothing, female voice used by AI programs for decades. "He is in his quarters on board the

Sunburst Over Fuji which is docked in Dock Number 214 in Section C."

"And what is his current medical condition?"

"He is in stable condition, heart rate below normal, unconscious, blood pressure at 120 over 70 . . ."

Albert didn't know how bad that was. He wasn't that kind of doctor. But it didn't sound good. "Station, alert the security services and medical to send a team to *Sunburst Over Fuji* immediately. Lockdown the ship to preserve evidence."

Currnea was nodding. "I am ashamed of my role in this stabbing as well."

"Okay, explain to me how this happened in sequence. Captain Franzen disabled the cameras. You stabbed Miss Tiffany. Then you went back to the ship and stabbed Captain Franzen there?"

"Oh, no, you misunderstand. I stabbed Miss Tiffany while I was still on the ship with Captain Franzen, on my way here." She tapped a claw on the table. Albert had abandoned thinking of them as fingers. A claw. "Then Captain Franzen must have disabled the cameras. Then he killed Miss Tiffany. Then station security came to get me and brought me here. Then you were brought here. Here, I told you about Captain Franzen, so I stabbed him just moments ago."

"Wait, so Captain Franzen killed Miss Tiffany?"

"I assume so. I wasn't there when he did that, but I know I stabbed her."

"Currnea, please explain how you did this."

"I was supposed to meet with Miss Tiffany. I told that to Captain Franzen. I did not know. But knowing is my job. Knowing what to say and what to withhold. Just like

Miss Tiffany. But when I told him she and I have the same job, I stabbed her."

"You . . ." Albert struggled to find the words. He pointed at Currnea's claws. "You pushed those inside Miss Tiffany's chest and back thirty-seven times?"

"No. I never met Miss Tiffany. I told Captain Franzen Miss Tiffany and I are both translators. No, diplomats. No, spies. Salespeople? By telling Captain Franzen that Miss Tiffany was to be my contact, I revealed her job. I did not know that for you humans, part of being a translator is not telling people you are a translator. Miss Tiffany was a secret translator. She didn't just withhold information from clients to help negotiate sales. She withheld her role as a salesperson of information from clients. We Thetch do not do this. I'm not even sure how it would work. How do humans keep their jobs secret and perform those jobs?"

"Fuck," Albert said, and smiled.

"I don't understand. You are expressing anger and happiness?"

"I am relieved that my confusion has been assuaged and angry at myself for not understanding sooner. You have been very clear, Currnea. I didn't understand. This is my fault. You see, when you used the word "stabbed" to describe your actions towards a person who was literally stabbed, I thought you stabbed her. Physically."

"I did."

"Wait, what?"

"You say she was stabbed. Physically. Her skin was punctured. I caused this to happen. So I stabbed her."

"Currnea, did you push your fingers into Miss Tiffany's skin?"

"No. I caused Captain Franzen to kill Miss Tiffany.

He didn't know she was a translator. He did know her, and he had revealed information to her. I expect it had to do with who his passengers were. It can be very valuable, in a negotiation, to know who other potential buyers might be. I often do not make others aware that I am a potential buyer in a negotiation. But I am always a translator. Miss Tiffany was a secret translator. When Captain Franzen learned she was a translator, through my stabbing, he became angry with Miss Tiffany. He attempted to withhold this information from me, but I could read his anger. When the police arrived in my room and told me Miss Tiffany had been killed, I knew I'd stabbed her. And by telling you Captain Franzen killed her, I've stabbed him, too."

Albert slowly reached his hand across the table. "May I place my hand on your hand, Currnea? This is a human gesture of comfort."

"You may," she said.

He patted her hand. It felt like hardened leather or plastic, but the little hairs tickled. "Please be assured, Currnea, you have done nothing wrong. You didn't kill anyone. Captain Franzen will be punished for his own choice to kill Miss Tiffany. You didn't choose to kill anyone."

"Now I am confused," Currnea said. Under his palm, he could feel her fingers tapping on the table, trying to calculate. "I cannot meet with my contact because she is dead. She died painfully. I have failed in my mission, and I have caused that painful death. I am ashamed that I have failed, and that I caused pain and death." She looked up at the ceiling. Then she lowered her head and stared hard into Albert's eyes. Or, at least, he felt she was staring hard. "Yet you say I should not feel ashamed, even though my words, my errors, my giving of information I should not have given, this failure of my job, has caused these effects. Why should I not be ashamed?"

"Because you didn't intend to cause these effects."

"I fail to see how my intentions are relevant to my responsibility," Currnea said.

"Humans often ascribe responsibility based on intent rather than impact."

"But why?"

"I cannot defend it," Albert said. "It's not a very good system."

For more of Benjamin Gorman's worlds, head to www.teachergorman.com.

THE SMUGGLER

A LADY HELLGATE SHORT STORY

BY GREG DRAGON

WHEN IT CAME TO SMUGGLING CARGO, THERE WERE
three basic rules. Deliver on time, deliver discreetly, and
the most important of the three: never open the package.
For as long as Maysun Sear had been running goods from
Nova Mar Station, he had committed to these rules, and
that in turn afforded him the privilege of the best paying
hauls.

That wasn't to say he was never curious, but the rules
were strict, and if you were caught violating them, there
went your career and your life. Maysun, who graduated
from selling stims and hacking personal storage caches,
knew better than most the value of this job. Smuggling
was dangerous, yes, but the credits earned would allow
him to move his family from a crowded hub to a spacious
compartment in the Nusalein Cluster. Now that would
be a success story.

A smile found his face as he thought about traveling
with his beloved, Suri Ola, and fulfilling his promise of
showing her the galaxy from the decks of a merchant class

hauler. She had been patient with him for years. Risking her life to join him on a station where she had no friends or family, only him.

He surveyed his class-2 freighter, *Tipsy Darling*, hearing the squeaks and groans from the imperfections throughout her 45m length. Part of her cockpit was dead from an electrical failure, and she had no FTL drive — which made her affordable but restricted Maysun's travel to the Genesian system, which in turn kept him out of the running on several jobs.

"Soon," he promised himself, "we'll get a new rig, something fast and safe for my Suri Ola."

He looked over the starmap, bopping the console twice with his fist to steady the stuttering holo threatening to go out. Like most hub dwellers, Maysun knew electronics and how to cross wires, but even he was starting to worry that his self-taught expertise was not enough to keep his junker afloat.

"Three cycles to go," he breathed, placing his feet up on the console and rocking back to the lowest decline the chair would allow. "Three lonely cycles," he sighed, suddenly feeling restless.

Unbuckling his restraints, he stood up and stretched, his knuckles brushing the low overhead of the flight deck. Flinching visibly, he glanced up to make sure he hadn't dislodged anything important. There hadn't been enough panels salvaged from his last run to repair the *Tipsy Darling's* exposed bulkheads.

"Soon," he made himself promise again, but something appeared on the starmap, interrupting his thoughts.

Three white blobs glowed on the edge of the holographic simulation, growing into four, five, six, until it appeared as a fleet dropping out of light speed. Maysun stood frozen for a long time watching them approach, but a shriek from the console brought his attention to the comms. He was being hailed through an open channel, and when he saw the Alliance's signature, he knew that he was in trouble.

"Freighter, this is Lieutenant Paola Cox of the Starlance Squadron. You are operating in restricted Alliance space. Exit immediately. Do you copy?" announced a stern voice that reminded him of Suri's mother, a woman who made his life hell back when they lived on the planet Genese.

"Copy that, Lieutenant, I will exit immediately," Maysun nearly shouted into the receiver after finding his voice. Sitting back heavily in his chair, his trembling right hand reached forward to take the controls while his left danced across the navigation screen, plotting a course out of the zone.

"Hold, freighter," came that alto again, locking him down in much the same way it did whenever he was confronted by Suri's raging matriarch. His blood turned to ice, causing him to sit back with his eyes wide and dry as he stared out the canopy into space.

He couldn't see them with his naked eyes but could imagine the lieutenant and her fleet, closing in on his vector at an increased thrust. A flawless record of smuggling runs was about to be over. *But why?* he wondered. *Had the officer picked up something in my voice?* He could never know. Whatever it was, he knew her telling him to "hold" was a death sentence, one many smugglers recounted hearing before being boarded and slapped into stasis cuffs.

A prompt on the heads-up display revealed a scan being conducted on his freighter, and he knew the results would come up as suspicious, prompting an immediate investigation. Desperate and frightened, Maysun weighed his options, even considering the absurd, like relinquishing the haul to have it drift away to where no one would ever find it. Rage replaced fear, and he punched the console, recoiling from the pain, as he examined the extent of damage to his freshly bruised knuckles.

"Freighter, power down your engine and prepare to be boarded," the lieutenant ordered, with a hint of annoyance. Maysun complied by killing the thrust, but kept the generator running to build up energy—just in case. The thought of losing everything he'd worked for filled his head with schemes to evade the Alliance.

Two vessels were indeed at max thrust heading his way. A fighter and an assault cruiser he knew would carry a team of Marines, who would board and search his vessel for contraband. Maysun reasoned that at the rate they were traveling, he would have a little under thirty minutes to come up with a plan. He made his way towards the stern, where the crate he was smuggling sat among fuel reserves he had picked up at Nova Mar Station.

If I'm going down for this, I may as well learn what it is before they do, he thought, and though it killed him to break one of his work's stringent rules, he found it in himself to crack open the crate. If he made it out he would make up a lie to tell the client, but perhaps this was all for nothing. There could be something the Alliance wouldn't care about inside the crate.

The lid slid open to reveal a large, pyramid-shaped holo-emitter, and he placed it on a shelf to trigger the playback. The emitter projected a hologram from the tip, which shimmered and solidified into the Anstractor Alliance's symbol—an "A" split in half by the thrust of a stylized starship. Below it appeared a series of glyphs, Maysun recognized as ancient Vestalian. "Property of the Anstractor Alliance," they read, which may as well have translated to: "If you're not Alliance and you have this, you are in trouble."

That's it, they're putting me out the airlock, he worried. *Why would someone do this? Have me transporting Alliance assets? This will be considered treason if I'm caught.*

"*Thype!*" he cursed aloud in frustration.

The Alliance symbol vanished to be replaced by a starmap, showcasing the location of Alliance vessels throughout the galaxy. With a gesture of his hand, Maysun found that he could zoom in on any area to get the details on a planet, moon, or vessel. He could imagine every capital ship having a similar emitter, but why was this one being shipped away, locked inside a crate?

An alarm began to blare, warning of an Extra-Dimensional Shift happening in the system. Maysun whispered a prayer. An EDS could happen anywhere, and *Tipsy Darling* didn't have the software needed to take evasive measures. All he could do was pray it wouldn't happen near his location, where he could disappear through the wormhole to maker knew where.

Running from window to window, he tried to deduce what was happening outside. Beyond the stars and line of lights from the distant fleet approaching Maysun couldn't see a thing, but in his gut he knew his eyes couldn't be trusted. With the thrusters off and the generator cooling, the silence of space was like a shroud, broken only by the tweets and beeps coming from the system.

"Freighter," that stern voice again announced over the comms. "A transfer passage is being extended to your portside hatch, and a team is preparing to enter. We will require permission to look over your cargo. Compliance will be rewarded with expediency and allowance of passage through this space. Captain, do we have your consent to board and search your vessel?"

It was now or never, he realized, and upon hearing the sounds from the hatch he panicked, his survival instinct triggered, putting all thoughts of commiseration out of his mind. He picked up the holo-emitter, powered it off, and grabbed an unopened crate filled with ration bars, meal pellets, and drink pouches. Smugglers overpacked on purpose, given the unpredictable nature of Alliance-run space and the imperfections with the technology powering their vessels.

Maysun grabbed a pressurized blanket and his EVA suit before pulling the latch on the escape pod and throwing everything he carried inside. One final glance at the flight deck, and a silent apology to *Tipsy Darling* for what was to come, he climbed into the pod's belly where his suit and supplies lay scattered on the small, half-moon-shaped deck. Reaching up, he sealed the hatch and locked it. Anyone who wanted access from outside now would need to employ a torch. Over the comms, he heard the lieutenant repeat her question. There was a finality to her tone, and he accepted that he was now at a point of no return with his escape.

Knowing the Alliance fleet would be monitoring his systems, Maysun dared not power on the pod. Now it was a matter of waiting for an opportunity to make an escape. Worst case scenario, they would track him leaving, and one of their fighters would likely disable his thrusters and haul him in to answer for his resistance. Best case scenario, he would drift away into space while they tore apart *Tipsy Darling* looking for his hiding place.

The escape pod was a custom addition that had been a black-market installment. Everything worked, but only from the console, not through the freighter's system like conventional pods. Maysun hoped this and its small size would make it invisible to tactical radar. He sat staring into nothing for what felt like an eternity, with his only source of light being the illuminated release valve on the hatch.

Maysun's chest felt ready to burst, and his throat constricted, making him suspicious that the pod wasn't providing him with sufficient oxygen. Aside from this was his anxiety, the guilt of taking this job, getting caught, and leaving Suri behind. He felt foolish, like one of those thrust heads hanging about the docks on Nova Mar Station, recalling their last run which eventually led to their ruin. Ironically this was the most unbearable of his emotions in that instance. He didn't want to be detained, just to show up ten years later, bent, broken, and alone.

Way to throw everything away, idiot, he thought, bitterly disappointed in himself. Even if he managed to make it out, he would be out of a ship and the client's cargo. Credits were low, and this score was supposed to be the rebound from a year's worth of debt. Going home empty-handed now and a wanted fugitive from the Alliance would be a life he would have to face alone. Suri was loyal, but he wouldn't put her through that, not after everything she had withstood for placing her trust in him.

The sound of hull-cutters broke the silence, droning on for nearly an hour while Maysun sat thinking about the past and decisions he had made. Credits had never come easy doing things the right way. Twenty credits a week for hauling miners could barely pay for a two-room shelter inside one of the settlements. Smuggling afforded he and Suri a modicum of dignity despite the risks. They no longer struggled to make ends meet, but he wanted to get his family off the planet. Suri would manage, he decided. She was like him: a Basce City homegrown, born hull tough and able to persevere.

Shouts from above, and Maysun knew the Marines had taken the deck. They would find it abandoned, but the seat warm and the comms channel open. As soon as they found the escape pod's hatch, he planned to launch and take his chances out in space.

Maysun leaned forward and placed his fingers on the console. The computer registered his ID and came to life, illuminating the space. He powered on the engines, placed them on standby, and eyed the comms for any new activity. He hoped nothing would be incoming since the pod's engines would be indistinguishable from the freighter to the Alliance's radar.

After five long minutes of watching his shaking fore-finger hover above the launch activation, Maysun accessed the *Tipsy Darling's* system to see what was happening on her decks. Black-clad Marines were inside every compartment, going through crates and rifling through storage. At the same time, a handful of less armored spacers probed the bulkheads, looking for what he assumed was his hiding place.

Seeing that none of the invaders were near the escape pod's hatch, Maysun chanced a glance at the cameras outside his vessel and was surprised to see a war being waged. Alliance phantoms jousted with Geralos zip-ships while the cruisers traded blows with a pair of dreadnoughts. Mis-fired energy rounds and laser traces danced dangerously close to *Tipsy Darling*, and panic threatened to overtake him, but he fought it down.

He knew then that the Extra-Dimensional Shift from earlier had been a Geralos fleet jumping into the system, where the Alliance fleet was waiting with torpedoes loaded. *And I thought I was having a rotten day*, Maysun thought with some amusement. The Geralos were a reptilian race of fanatics who tore apart the galaxy looking for human brains to consume. Maysun had never seen one of these horrors but heard enough tales to know what to expect should he get captured by them.

Switching the feed to inside his vessel, he saw a change in the Marines' demeanor. It was as if a switch had been flipped, sending them scrambling to escape *Tipsy Darling's* decks. Maysun couldn't see the warnings they received of an incoming torpedo from the Geralos dreadnought with no tactical radar on either console. The impact knocked him unconscious when it struck, as the escape pod was thrown from the explosion to hurdle unchecked away into space.

When Maysun came awake, he was floating and so thrown off by his position that he flailed about screaming, thinking he had died, and what he was experiencing was the void before oblivion. Headache aside, his rational brain eventually picked up on the fact that he was still living, but the sudden loss of gravity meant the pod was no longer attached to the freighter. He was breathing, so the oxygen worked, and where his legs dangled, he saw the twinkling blue lights of power moving about the compartment.

Now that he'd managed to get his bearings, Maysun reached up to touch at his face. He felt the back of his head, and finally the scalp, looking for the source of his soreness. He located the area above his right ear, where his head had snapped down from the torpedo's impact that had pulled apart his ship. Maysun reasoned that the pod's flawed attachment was the only reason why he survived. His scalp was tender and throbbed with pain, but he didn't find any blood, and his sense of place was returning. The small compartment was all-white, well-illuminated, but messy with all the items he had thrown in when he used it to hide.

Reaching for his bulky EVA suit, he climbed through the top and activated the pressure valve to suck out the excess air. The EVA clung to his form snugly and did wonders for his conscience now that his body was no longer exposed. Twisting his body to catch the floating helmet, Maysun grabbed a handhold and maneuvered himself to the console, which took some effort. A practiced kick got him into the chair, where he found the restraints, snapped them taut, and took a moment to exhale. Now for the moment of truth, he thought, dreading what he would find once he powered on the computer to learn its status. *Better to just rip the bandaging off.* He touched the activation icon, putting on a brave face as the holographic display appeared.

"I've been out for a couple of hours," he mused, "Still near the fighting, but none of them are coming after me. *Thype* my luck, *Tipsy Darling's* gone without a trace. She must've been hit, and . . . and my pod survived." He felt the weight of his mortality, and for the first time in his 28 years, it altered the way he saw himself. Suddenly time no longer felt finite, and he was free from all the pressure and obligations.

Maysun accepted that he should have died along with

his freighter, but now that he had survived, he would need to contact someone willing to send some help. The pod had enough energy reserved to get back to the Nusalein Cluster but making it there could take up to two years. Pods were meant for rescue, not for space travel, and he dared not consult the radio until he was beyond the possibility of interference from the Geralos.

He wondered how the Alliance was faring against their attackers and the chances of his pod making it far enough to be out of range of the fleet. Grudgingly he glanced over at the holo-emitter, wondering how he could charge the client ten times more if he still managed to make the delivery.

Now that he knew what he carried, he considered all the options that could benefit him. If he contacted the Alliance, he could turn himself in and admit to having in his possession a holo-emitter with their secrets. They, of course, would want to know the client and the intended destination, which, after haggling a reward, he would happily tell them. They would have to promise him no prison time and enough credits to replace his old ship. If they refused that, he would demand that they relocate his entire family. *But, will the Alliance be flexible?* he wondered.

What could come from that, besides a handful of credits and a junker that would break apart in light speed? He only could imagine. At least the Alliance believed in honor. He was used to working with predators, who filed their teeth on the credits they grifted. Studying the starmap, Maysun surmised that it would be a Vestalian week's time before he was far enough out of range to send an SOS.

If he were lucky, the Genesian Guard would conduct

the rescue, and he would make up a story about losing his ship to pirates. He made himself a promise that if he survived, this would be his last haul as a smuggler. The emitter would be his undoing, but Maysun expected to get something for his effort. Still, he would need another stroke of luck with whoever he chose to exchange it with for credits.

He busied himself making plans for several days while he chewed on ration bars and drank vitamin water from sealed, vacuum-friendly packets. When he grew bored, he consulted the holo-emitter, studying the known galaxy and the multitude of starships. Being alone inside the escape pod made Maysun reflect on things he harbored but refused to confront in the past. Like draining their savings to repair *Tipsy Darling* with hopes of repaying it once the package had been delivered.

He was a liar with no legacy to leave behind and no credits to aid his wife in adjusting to his absence. How had he not seen this coming, planned contingencies, and done the bare minimum required of a provider in a dangerous profession?

Thoughts of doom, solitude, and the constant beeping from the console sent his mind through a gauntlet of paranoia and confusion. Maysun eventually lost track of time, his grandiose plans for fencing the emitter no longer present. His thoughts dwelled somewhere in a dimension between reality and dreams, where time was inconsequential. He kept playing back the last argument he'd had with Suri concerning her parents.

She had wanted them closer, but Maysun argued that he couldn't afford to pay for the trip. She, in turn, had mentioned his gambling and paying the fines that came from his drunken shenanigans. Each time he replayed the argument, he corrected his answers to minimize her anger. He got it to the point where she complimented him for "seeing things clearly," and he was able to pull her in for an embrace.

He played it over, skipping forward each time to start closer to where the last replay ended. The only break he received from this exercise was when his stomach would force him to consume a ration. Six days in and Maysun returned to the present, and it felt as if he'd woken up from the most peaceful sleep. He was unaware of how much time had passed until he rubbed at his neck and felt the beginnings of a beard.

Confused and frightened, Maysun looked to the console, which displayed a holographic simulation of the pod and the area around it. He saw that he was now tethered to a vessel large enough to be a cruiser or a dreadnought. He'd manage to escape only to fall into the clutches of a warship that was likely part of the fleet he was fleeing. Maysun touched a few options to place the system's focus on his captor and panned out far enough to get an idea of the type of ship. He instantly recognized the shape as an older dreadnought, developed by his ancestors as a premier fighting fortress in the Galactic War.

A Genesian ship meant Alliance spacers, and he exhaled with some relief, knowing he wouldn't die and would have time to plead his case. If he could sell them on the story he had practiced, he might get a new ship or a commendation. The most important thing was that he would be alive and could find a way to contact Suri.

He had given it his all and had survived the crossfire of a full-fledged Alliance and Geralos engagement. Even from a cell, no one would be able to match his tale of running contraband past an Alliance blockade, getting caught, then using a rigged escape pod to get away. Still, no hail came from the Alliance vessel, which Maysun found peculiar, but he reasoned that they wouldn't be pleased if the dreadnought belonged to the fleet he initially escaped.

He could hear sounds from outside, then felt a sudden shift in the pod's trajectory. Another shift and his shoulder struck the console, inadvertently maxing the thrust, which swung the pod in another direction, breaking his restraints to send him crashing into the bulkhead. Maysun powered down the engine to allow his captors to apply a tractor beam to reel him in. More violent jerks from without, followed by silence, and the dreadnought's artificial gravity took hold, allowing him to stand and rub at his wounds.

The hatch was coming open, so he located the emitter, picked it up, and held it close to his chest. "I am the victim here," he recited. Taking deep breaths to get into the character of a down-and-out spacer, grateful to be rescued but loathe to separate from his emitter, the last remnant of his disabled ship. That was the story he'd practiced but wrongly assumed he'd have time to master.

The hatch came open, and with it, a smell worse than anything he'd ever experienced followed by a thick cloud of something that quickly poured into the compartment. On instinct, Maysun reached for his helmet, pulled it on, and activated the seal. The cloud came in thickly, sticking to the bulkhead, his EVA suit, and anything unlucky enough to be in its way. Everything became covered in a thick layer of spores, which continued to pour in relentlessly.

Maysun kept wiping at the glass of his helmet to see

what was coming. He could barely make out the three figures that followed, coming down the ladder and pulling him out into what appeared to be the galaxy's filthiest hangar. His helmet was removed, quite aggressively, and he came face-to-face with what he would describe as a humanoid face, with scaly skin that was void of nose and lips.

What frightened him the most were the eyes. There were no pupils, just a deep, black pool that looked to hold their own cruel galaxies inside their depths. Here was a Geralos, the last encounter Maysun expected coming from the signature of a Genesian ship. He hadn't considered that the Geralos, or "lizards" as they were slurred by Alliance spacers and loyalists, could capture a prized vessel and convert it for their own schemes. He had been so sure he was getting rescued, only to again face certain death, and this time he wasn't confident there would be a way out.

Spores were everywhere, and he had been a second too late in donning his helmet. The ones he ingested elicited a cough followed by the contents of his stomach. Maysun fell to his knees, where he continued to retch, thinking it to be fatal and hoping it would be quick to spare him from whatever the Geralos planned for him. Two strong arms pulled him back to his feet, struck him across the face, knocking him unconscious, and he was suddenly back on Nova Mar Station, at a fruit stand with Suri bartering prices.

He knew it was a dream but couldn't recall how he got there, all thoughts of his life gone within the dream's dimension. Again, Maysun refined his memories with every playback, so immersed that he began to no longer see them as dreams.

The chill of the compartment finally roused him, and he awoke to a searing pain throughout his limbs. His hands were bolted to the bulkhead above his head, high enough to where his toes barely touched the deck. It was a torment to his arms, which felt dislocated, but it was so cold he found it hard to think, let alone focus on the pain. All he could manage was to wail through dried, cracked lips into the silence of that dark space.

He guessed that he had been placed in storage, like frozen meat or like the many ration bars that had sustained him in the escape pod. Like those supplements, at some point, a Geralos would come in, pull him down and devour his brains. Maysun had no way of knowing how long he'd been under before waking up inside what-ever this was. He could hear the hum of a crystal core generator, and that told him he was indeed still on board the Genesian-built dreadnought.

Had he the strength or the training, he would have found a way to slip his chains, find another escape pod, and give escape another try. However, this time he would have no leverage, no holo-emitter to guarantee the help of the Alliance. The most he could win was more time with his Suri. But, considering what would happen if he went back there empty-handed, he would be better off dying and removing any connection she had with the smuggler's ring.

There were three rules for smuggling cargo: deliver on time, deliver discreetly, and never open the package. Maysun may have broken the first, but so did many in his profession, he reasoned. The ones who lived to explain why had always relayed the critical situations that warranted it. Maysun could now count himself among their number, though survival at this point was yet another fever dream.

The package had been opened, and he had held onto it until the very end. Perhaps if he had the vocal anatomy to speak the Geralos language, he could have found a way to reason with them. He was smuggling Alliance secrets, and who would be the buyer? Wouldn't it be the Geralos, or someone deeply affiliated with them? Having seen the contents of the holo-emitter, he believed he had inadvertently made the delivery.

Once they discovered what he had, the contract would have been filled, and his run had been a success despite the damage to the Alliance it presented. Could he hope that the client would learn of them having it and send the credits to his account, where Suri could access it?

There was also the chance that an Alliance ship could intercept the dreadnought and reclaim their property. Whatever would come, Maysun had already made peace with his misgivings, accepting that his run had, in fact, been a success. He had managed to deliver every package in a lengthy career. No one would know except the Geralos and his client, but that was enough for him.

Maysun Sear, husband, and smuggler closed his eyes and returned to the market. There he would remain, too far gone to know or care what happened to his body. He wouldn't feel the Geralos's teeth pierce his brain, but he would feel Suri's hand as they walked, speaking of a future he would never see.

"The Smuggler" takes place in the Lady Hellgate universe. For more adventures in the galaxy of Anstractor, read Last of the Nighthawks (*Lady Hellgate book* 1) *by Greg Dragon.*

And don't miss The Judas Cypher, *available for free on all platforms.*

HIGHLY IRREGULAR

A PARSE GALAXY SHORT STORY

BY KATE SHEERAN SWED

In Sloane's opinion, there was nothing more annoying than a space battle.

She had no business sitting here in the co-pilot seat during one, even though the *Moneymaker* technically belonged to her. But that was where she'd landed when the shooting had started, so that was where she was currently gripping the arms and trying—admirably, in her opinion—not to throw up.

Throwing up would probably distract Hilda. The pilot might be an ace, but some things were un-ignore-able. That apparently didn't include her green parakeet, which was fluttering back and forth on the dashboard, but it would definitely include vomit.

The ship banked sharply, making Sloane deeply regret the extra mayo she'd dolloped onto her veggie burger at lunch. Angry red slashes of plasma danced by the window, ricocheting off the *Moneymaker*'s shield, and she couldn't help but notice the movement of the dial at Hilda's elbow. Helpfully labeled 'shield integrity,' it dropped its arrow out of the green zone — a universal indication of safety, as far as Sloane knew — and into a suspiciously orange-colored one.

What was the point in whipping the ship around like this if they were going to get hit, anyway?

"This is getting old," Sloane said.

Hilda hit a button and the ship plummeted. Space was sadly lacking in 'up' and 'down,' but it *felt* like plummeting, which was all that mattered. Sloane had no way to tell if the plummeting actually accomplished anything; the shield arrow quivered, but it didn't drop any further.

"Oh, I'm sorry," Hilda said. "Am I messing up your hair as I *try to save our lives?*"

"Yeah, actually, but that's not really my priority right now."

"Glad to hear it."

The ship shuddered, and the shield integrity arrow swooped toward the always-dangerous red zone.

"I hope Alex strapped in," Sloane said. Their third crew member, a scientist, had a tendency to forget her surroundings when she got lost in her work.

"Not going to matter in another second."

The good news: most of the ships that'd been following them for the last week, taking occasional potshots without actually trying to kill them, had peeled off a few hours ago.

The bad news: there was one ship left, and it seemed to be holding a grudge.

The worst news: it also seemed to know the truth. That Sloane and her crew had instigated a wild goose chase, and that the treasure their attackers dearly wanted was not technically in residence.

And if the straggler knew *that*, then they were *definitely* trying to blow up the ship in earnest.

"You pretend to steal one little artifact and everyone goes nuts," Sloane said.

"No good deed goes unpunished," Hilda said.

Since it'd been Sloane's good deed to divert attention by pretending to steal the artifact — one she'd taken on without consulting her crew — the words felt a bit like an accusation.

Not that now was the time to dwell on other people's hang-ups.

Sloane made herself lean forward so she could look out and catch a glimpse of their attacker. The mean little ship was circling them like a shark. Its next bite would take a chunk out of the *Moneymaker* for sure.

"Remind me why we're not shooting back," Sloane said, allowing the barest thread of accusation to leak into her tone.

Hilda rolled her eyes, along with the ship — Sloane's stomach did a somersault, and she swallowed hard — and pointed to a bar that displayed one cheerful green square. "See how only one square is lit up there? We've got one plasma round left, and their shields are at one hundred percent."

"So basically, we dance until we die."

"Basically."

Ignoring her stomach's pleas, Sloane forced herself to take a look out the strip of window she'd been ignoring up until now. She watched as their pursuer launched another angry red wad of laser fire at the ship.

She didn't understand much about space battles and shooting things. But it seemed to her that there was one very obvious question that no one ever mentioned.

"How do their plasma shots get past *their* shield?" Sloane asked.

"What?"

Sloane pointed, though it was hardly necessary. Or helpful. "Why can a ship's guns blast past the shield? Shouldn't the shot rebound back into the ship?"

Sloane wasn't sure how to read Hilda's silence. She might've been stunned at Sloane's ignorance, or praying for a competent co-pilot to pop up in her place. It was hard to tell.

"I don't actually know," the pilot said finally.

Had Sloane not been strapped into her chair, she'd have fallen out of it.

"So," she said, "couldn't we shoot at the guns? Like down the barrel of those cannons?"

Hilda's jaw twitched just enough for Sloane to suspect she was grinding her teeth. "We have *one* full plasma chamber. That's it."

"So let's use it."

"We'd have to position the ship *directly* at the end of their cannon. The one that's currently trying to blow us into dust."

"But you know how long it takes them to switch plasma chambers when they drain their ammo. Don't you?"

Hilda shot her a look of disdain. "I'm a trained fighter pilot, girl. Of course I know."

"Well?"

"Six seconds."

Not as long as she'd have hoped, but Sloane figured they could work with that. More or less. When in doubt, it was better not to do the math in situations like this. "Then we get them to shoot at us until they spend their round, then we line up and shoot them in the guns."

Sloane had said her fair share of strange sentences, but that one ranked pretty high.

Hilda cursed under her breath. "This is a terrible idea."

"I'm good for those."

The parakeet hopped onto Hilda's shoulder, as if for moral support. And then they were off.

It was a good thing, Sloane thought, that Hilda was an excellent pilot. No, she was an *ace* pilot. A champion racer, an ex-fighter, a woman who'd been zipping around the Parse Galaxy since well before Sloane's birth.

Gravity fritzed as Hilda spun the *Moneymaker* in a zig-zagging spiral, flying it like an extension of her own skin. Even when death was imminent, the pilot flew with a little smile on her lips.

If this scheme failed, Sloane suspected Hilda might just die happy.

Sloane, on the other hand, would die pissed off.

The ship they faced was just like any other random, non-luxury ship in the galaxy: slate gray siding, big ugly bolts everywhere, and a mean-looking cannon jutting out the side. The gun was so big, it almost looked like *Moneymaker* could fly right down the barrel.

Not that Sloane would have suggested that.

When Hilda reeled around, Sloane's stomach slingshotted into her throat. And then, eerily, everything paused.

The moment shouldn't have been any different from the rest of the cat-and-mouse battle they'd been engaged in. It wasn't like space was *more* silent when a ship stopped shooting, beyond the fact that it stopped the *Moneymaker* from shuddering and knocking pictures off the walls or whatever.

This moment felt different, though. Maybe it was because they'd pulsed to a stop directly in front of the cannon, and it felt like looking into the mouth of a tooth-less shark.

Moneymaker's shot hit its target dead center, and Sloane just had time to see a flash of blue from inside as the other ship lobbed off a desperate last round, but it was too late; the shots collided, and Hilda was already speeding away to avoid the debris as their attacker exploded.

"That is a major loophole," Sloane said, breathing hard. "They really should fix it."

"I'm probably the only pilot in the Parse Galaxy who had a chance of pulling that off," Hilda said.

The ship shuddered, and the helpful shield arrow dropped into the angry red zone. A dozen alarms startled into screams as debris slammed into the *Moneymaker*, peppering its sides with the remains of its enemies.

What a way to go.

"Almost," Hilda said. "I almost pulled it off."

Sloane didn't know how to feel about the fact that the closest station was a friendly, law-abiding kind of place.

On one hand, the Indly Station crew welcomed the hobbling *Moneymaker* with sympathetic tsks and mugs of tea. Which was a nice change from most of the places Sloane had frequented lately.

On the other hand, though, law-abiding places were not the best option for finding jobs that could fund expensive repairs.

Needless to say, she didn't sleep well. And since the

shower cyclers were among the damaged systems, she couldn't even wash away the battle with a hot scrub.

Sloane found Alex and Hilda in the former security officer's cabin, huddled over his tablet. Hilda's parakeet flew lazy circles above their heads as they scrolled.

Nothing they found here would do them any good.

Sloane hadn't entered Oliver's room since the crew had returned to the *Moneymaker* without their former security officer. Hadn't thought much of him, in general. They'd been . . . whatever they'd been. Colleagues with benefits, at the least. Falling in love at the most, maybe. Or so she'd thought, until he'd betrayed their trust. Talk about a fraud.

She hesitated in the doorway, watching her crewmates. Hilda looked rested enough, but Alex hadn't been the same since their last adventure had destroyed her life's work.

The scientist wore the same graying sweatshirt she'd had on for the last week, and her red hair was a tangle that hadn't seen a brush in at least as long. Sloane thought there might be gum stuck in the back. Even her bunny slippers were gray with dirt and food stains.

Sloane didn't understand it, really. So wormholes were too unstable and dangerous to pursue. So they could rip apart the fabric of reality and the universe as they knew it. So achieving one had been the work of Alex's last decade or so.

Alex was a scientist. Surely she could find something else to work on.

Sloane cleared her throat. "Do I need to remind you two what happened to the last guy on this ship who took on the kinds of jobs you're looking at right now?"

Hilda glanced over her shoulder at Sloane. "We're

only looking at legitimate Cosmic Trade Federation-approved listings," she said. "I doubt Oliver's job was stamped."

No, it definitely hadn't been. "Bounties?" Sloane asked.

Hilda's nod was a businesslike twitch of her chin. She tapped a finger on the screen. "This one pays well."

"Then we probably can't handle it."

"It's the only job available out here," Alex said.

Sloane sighed. A bounty hunt was probably the best way to secure a wad of cash quickly, and she didn't really want to spend months slinging drinks or shining shoes out here just to slap a few cheap band-aids on the hulls.

They needed actual repairs, and they needed them now. She couldn't keep shuffling her own mission off to the side; it was just too obvious that she didn't belong here. The sooner they repaired the *Moneymaker*, the sooner she could find her uncle and return his ship to him. Along with its crew. He was the leader they needed, not Sloane.

She had to get back to her own life, her studies. If the medical school would even readmit her after she'd disappeared without a trace.

"All right," Sloane said, "I guess we'll handle it."

TUCKED SAFELY within one of the smaller middle systems in the Parse Galaxy, Indly Station must've had a dearth of bounty-oriented individuals, because the lister contacted them immediately.

By showing up at the *Moneymaker*'s dock.

"You didn't say he was *at* the station," Sloane said.

She was having to rearrange her whole idea of how a hunter actually discovered and set out on a bounty. She'd thought the details might be listed in full on the database, and that multiple hunters might compete to find the prize.

Or, failing that, that they'd receive a clandestine message through the boards. Possibly one they — or specifically Alex — would need to decrypt.

When she shared that guess, however, Alex just said, "I'm an astrophysicist. Not a computer scientist."

In any case, the person tottering around the dock was an elderly man, his back just a little bent, the skin on his neck just a little droopy. He had tufts of gray hair patched onto his skull at seemingly random intervals, giving the impression of a kid's craft project — Sloane's little sister would have placed the hair more regularly — and a cane with a silver goose on the top.

Which he was currently using to tap at the *Money-maker*'s sides, punctuating each blow with a dissatisfied grunt. As if banging metal could really tell him whether the ship was about to fall apart.

At least, she didn't think it could.

"I don't think we're going to get this job," Sloane said.

"Not unless you go out and talk to him, we're not," Hilda replied.

Sloane glanced at her. "I thought you were going to talk to him."

"You're the captain."

"You found the job."

Sloane had yet to win a staring match with Hilda, but that fact hadn't stopped her from trying. The old man tapped at the hull again, and she heard a part dislodge and crash to the ground. Whatever it was, it sounded expensive.

"I'm the pilot," Hilda said. "I already have a job."

Point taken. Sloane left the pilot's deck and descended to the cargo area, where she had to wriggle the code box violently to get the gangplank to fall open.

"This ship couldn't make it to the pee room, let alone another system." The man's dry rasp of a voice floated up from underneath *Moneymaker*'s belly, where she could hear his cane still tapping at the hull.

Sloane hated him already.

She bent over, trying to find where her potential customer — client? — was hiding. "You might be surprised."

The man hobbled out from under the ship. "I'm never surprised. But you're the only one who answered the ad. So we'd best get talking." He started up the gangplank without an invitation. "I'm assuming you've got some bore-hide tea in there somewhere?"

AFTER SETTLING for lavender-mint tea and settling himself at the head of the banged-up table in the galley, the man introduced himself as Curtis Corbin. The name fit him in a way names rarely fit people; it was a crushed accordion of a name, the hard consonants overtaking the vowels like they might collapse in on themselves the next time someone dared utter them.

"What's the job?" Sloane asked him as he slurped his tea.

He squinted at her. "Didn't you read the listing?"

"Nope. Picked it by location."

Curtis Corbin grated out a laugh. "And the money, no doubt."

"Didn't hurt. What's the job?"

He stirred his tea, coy, like he might not explain. Except that he'd already told her that no one else had responded. So Sloane just waited until he said, "It's a rescue operation. Orbiting prison."

"Who's the prisoner?"

"A friend."

"I love it when people give the full details."

Curtis looked at Hilda. "She always this charming?"

Hilda leaned her elbows on the table. "You caught her on a good day."

Alex, who was leaning in the door frame—bunny slippers and all—just snorted.

Sloane ignored the comment. And the snort. "Why can't the Fleet help? Because if he's *in* a Fleet prison, you can forget it. Those guys never forget."

Curtis grunted. "Savvier than you look, girl. It's not a Fleet prison, and they've been informed. But they've got a lot on their plate right now, not much interest in rescuing a single unfortunate."

Not a Fleet prison. OK, so far, so good. The Fleet supposedly linked the Parse Galaxy systems. They kept the peace. Or so they liked to think. They'd gotten in her way before; she was pretty sure they were destined to do it again.

"If it's not a Fleet prison," Sloane said, "then where is it?"

"Adu System. Been orbiting Izo's smallest moon for a decade now."

Sloane was on her feet before she'd entirely realized

she was moving. "The Bone System? No, no way. Forget it."

She'd sling drinks for a year to avoid that place. Not a chance.

Curtis raised his hands. They had a small tremor to them. "Calm, girl. It's not common knowledge, but *he's* not been seen in weeks. He's abandoned the system."

Didn't Sloane know it. She'd just escaped the last of *his* ships after guiding them on a wild goose chase. And after leading him to wreak havoc on a planet in an entirely different galaxy.

Accidentally, sure. But still.

"Call me 'girl' again and I'll rip out the rest of your hair," Sloane said.

Curtis Corbin leaned forward. "Think about it. Trade's been diverted around Adu System for over a century. Now that Sever's gone? Well, it's about to be the wild west again. I need to get my friend out of there."

No wonder he couldn't find anyone else to take this job. Sever fancied himself a demi-god. A reclusive one that resurfaced every now and then to respond to a perceived insult by annihilating entire planets. He was a genocidal horror show.

But Sloane knew what no one else did: that Sever really *had* left the galaxy, at least for a brief time. And if her friends in the Milky Way handled things — she wasn't much of an optimist, but she was rooting for them, anyway — maybe he'd stay gone.

In any case, they had some time. This *was* a Federation-stamped job, and if Sever was the one who'd incarcerated Curtis Corbin's friend, then he was very likely a good guy. Or at least, not a bad one.

It was a wonder that he was alive at all.

"I need seventy-five percent upfront," Sloane said.

Curtis puffed out a breath. "Not happening."

"Fifty."

"You new to this? You get paid when we win."

Sloane crossed her arms. "I can't fly my ship to your friend until it's repaired."

The old man squinted at the ceiling, as if he could read a full report of the necessary repairs there. "I'll get your ship moving," he said. "I'll pay the rest when my friend's free."

"And if we fail?"

"Well, I've never wanted a rust-bucket of a ship, but it'll do for collateral."

Rescue the friend, repair the ship, then fuel it so she could get back to her original mission of finding Uncle Vin.

Fail? Well, she could try to turn the ship over. But Uncle Vin had coded it to answer to Sloane alone. Alex, Hilda, and Oliver had all tried to work around it. Sloane had tried, too. To no avail.

The ship would only fly for Sloane. But Curtis Corbin didn't need to know that.

"OK," Sloane said. "What are we looking at?"

"Picture a walnut," Curtis Corbin said, "with a trio of shells protecting the meat."

"More like a torkfruit, then," Alex said.

Sloane shot the scientist a look, but Curtis nodded. "Just so. Picture a torkfruit. You need to crack through the outer shell and into the airlocks, through the airlock shell and into the main floor, then into the cell itself. Back out's a piece of cake."

Alex spun on her bunny-tailed heel and walked out of the kitchen.

Sloane glanced at Hilda. She was facing away from them, elbows on the counter, swiping through a holographic card game.

Sloane was clearly expected to be the mastermind here. "Guards?" she asked.

"Offsite. Since Sever disappeared, we don't know who's watching."

"No shields?"

He drew an imaginary whirlpool on the tabletop with his finger. "Shields activate if a ship comes within a certain range. We float in on our own, with rocket boosters."

"And carry extras for your friend."

Curtis rubbed his chin. "Precisely."

If Sloane planned to make a real go at this bounty hunter thing, she'd need to get better at reading people. Pull out her psychology class notes, at the very least. She couldn't decide if the prisoner was a lover of Curtis's, an associate, or someone who owed him money.

She wasn't sure she needed to know. Still, she couldn't help wishing she'd paid more attention to the way people interacted instead of honing now-useless skills, like the ability to spot a designer handbag from ten feet away.

"You don't have the airlock codes?" she asked.

"Correct."

Too much to hope for. "And we can't drill through without damaging the airlock and decompressing the rest of the station."

"Now you're getting it."

Sloane shook her head. "Not possible. You need armored guards or Fleet troops or . . ." Or someone who was competent. At *anything*.

Curtis didn't argue. He just sat back in his chair, the corners of his mouth drooping. She felt bad — about his friend, sure, and also about her money — but there wasn't anything she could do. Cracking through levels of a station without hacking it, or killing them all? It wasn't possible.

She supposed one of the nice people at Indly Station would agree to hire her as a bartender. Ironically, she made an excellent torkfruit cocktail.

Alex ambled back into the room, slippers shuffling on the floor, and dropped a silver tube on the table. It was covered in multicolored buttons, some large, some small. Knowing Alex's inventions as she did, Sloane had to fight the urge to scoot away from it.

"What is this?" she asked.

"Matter-phaser," Alex said, as if it should've been obvious. When Sloane just blinked, she picked it up, aimed it at the table, and pressed the biggest button at the end. The tube started to click, quickly at first, then winding down rapidly.

And then Alex stuck her fingers *through* the table.

Sloane blinked, her mind struggling to understand how Alex's fingers could be taking up the same space as the table. There wasn't a hole or a gap. There was table, and there were Alex's fingers. They couldn't be occupying the same space, she knew that. But they *looked* like they were occupying the same space.

"Matter-phaser," Alex said. She withdrew her fingers. "Just get your hand out before it stops clicking, or you'll lose it."

"It" being the hand, Sloane assumed, rather than the phaser.

Sloane hadn't thought Curtis Corbin was capable of

being impressed. At this demonstration, Sloane actually thought his beady little eyes might pop out and roll across the floor. "How many times will it work?" he asked.

"Three," Alex said. "Maybe four."

"I thought you said you were an astrophysicist, not an engineer," Sloane said.

Alex shrugged. "A person needs a hobby."

FROM A DISTANCE, the prison almost looked invisible. Even as Sloane got close, her boosters spitting sparks as they propelled her toward the station, she had to squint to make it out. The station was a smudge against the dark side of Izo's moon, a shadow tucked into the shadows. To her right, the rainbow glimmer of a current path promised a quick getaway. The currents kept traffic flowing around the Galaxy at near light speed, and it was hard to believe any of them cut this close to Sever's territory.

She might've passed within a few meters of the prison without realizing it was there, had she not been looking for it.

Sloane didn't like the fact that the *Moneymaker* was so far away, and Hilda with it. Out of reach, and unable to help if this went wrong.

They were only infiltrating a prison designed by a tyrant who considered himself a demi-god — or designed by his minions, at any rate. What could possibly go wrong?

Alex bobbed along to Sloane's right, still scowling at having been roosted from her room to help. If something went sideways with the matter-phaser, Sloane would be no good to anyone. She wasn't the kind of person to follow feverish instructions given through an earpiece while running from hypothetical enemies. Like hidden Fleet soldiers who turned out to be running the prison after all. Or Sever, back from the Milky Way to wreak vengeance on her.

Not that Sloane was imagining the various disasters they could be walking into.

Besides, Alex needed to leave that room. She was turning into a hermit.

Sloane was new to bounty hunting, but she didn't think it was typical for the client to come along on the job. Still, Curtis Corbin rocketed along to her left. Sloane didn't know if it was pain, age, or something else that curved his body into a C-shape as he moved through the vacuum, but she couldn't help wondering how the guy would get along on the station without his cane.

Maybe there wasn't any gravity. She could see Sever storing his hostages in a place like that.

Finally, they floated close enough to reach out and grab the airlock. Sloane glanced over her shoulder, but *Moneymaker* was far enough away that it was only a suggestion of a shape against the stars.

Curtis tapped the code box, and Alex dislodged the matter-phaser from her back. She aimed it at the door and nodded.

Sloane didn't like the feeling of being matter-phased, even with the protection of the atmo gear — what would happen if the matter-phaser phased the suit apart? — but she didn't have a choice. She reached in, her hand too bulky, and fumbled for the wires that powered the code box. Because it didn't matter if they tried to open the door from the inside if they still needed a code.

But the matter-phaser could phase them into the

middle of the airlock wall just as well as it could phase them all the way through.

"Just pull," Alex said, her voice tickling Sloane's ear as the bud vibrated.

"I need to cut them."

"How?"

"I have a retractable knife."

"You're wearing atmo gear. One puncture and you're done."

As if Sloane didn't know that. "What do you suggest?"

"I suggest you put your back into it and *pull*."

"Did you argue with my uncle like this?"

"Vincent didn't make dumb plans that would risk his life, so no."

Given that Uncle Vin had disappeared entirely, Sloane wasn't sure that was accurate. And would've said so, had Curtis not banged impatiently on the outside of the airlock.

Sloane gripped the bundle of wires as tightly as she could while wearing atmo gloves. And she pulled.

The wires snapped. The light on the code box blinked out. Sloane withdrew her hand from the wall, and when Alex lifted the latch, the door popped open.

Alex lifted an *I-told-you-so* eyebrow before slipping into the airlock, with Curtis right behind her.

The air cycled through, a second zap of the matter-phaser opened the next door, and artificial gravity pulled their boots to the floor.

As soon as her signals blinked green, Sloane lifted the visor on her helmet. Alex, meanwhile, left her visor firmly in place.

Beyond the airlock, the prison looked like a prison.

Sloane supposed she shouldn't have been surprised at that. She'd just sort of figured that it was bad enough to be stranded alone and orbiting a moon in the most feared section of the galaxy, with triple layers of security and no vessel to escape on. She'd figured even Sever would've given this guy the run of the place.

Clearly, though, the station had originally been intended for more occupants. The corridor looked too long for a station this size. Rust decorated the metal plates along the floor, and a series of iron doors made her wonder if Curtis's friend really was the only person trapped here.

Curtis Corbin limped out of the airlock and pushed past her. "Stop gawking and get a move on. He'll be in the center."

Sloane followed him down the hall. If there were other prisoners here, they stayed silent.

The door at the end of the hall was locked by yet another code box. Alex aimed the matter-phaser at the wall, and Sloane prepared to slip her fingers into the wall.

Nothing happened.

"You said it would work three times," Sloane said.

Alex put the phaser away. "What can I say? It's a prototype."

Curtis's eyebrows sank so low, they had to have been obscuring his vision. "You promised me—"

"Hold on," Sloane said. She ran her finger along the edge of the box until she found a sticker, then bent over and noted the module's serial number. She slid a fingernail around the side of the box and noted the sec code.

And, right below that, the speckled logo of the manufacturer.

"What are you trying to do, kiss the thing?" Curtis asked.

"I worked for a high-end boutique as a teenager," she said.

"And that helps us how?"

Sloane ignored the question and slipped her tab out of one of the interior pockets of the atmo suit to run a quick search. "Alex, what's the name of Sever's right-hand guy? It started with an M. Like Mordred. Or Molotov."

"Morik."

"Right." Sloane located the company, tapped the endlessly long call number — system area, planet, no moon extension, then local number — and waited.

"What are you doing?" Alex hissed.

But the other line went live, and Sloane held up a hand to silence her.

"Property Protect Limited mechanism department, how can I help you?" The representative's voice was high-pitched and syrupy sweet, no doubt trained to be.

"Oh, thank goodness," Sloane said. "I'm at box 87882, sec lock 778, and my code isn't working."

"Sorry to hear that, ma'am," the voice said. "But this is the mechanism department, not the security service line. Let me transfer you to — "

"No, you can't," Sloane interrupted. "*They* transferred me to *you*. They said the code was right, and it's not working, so it must be a box malfunction."

A beat of silence. "They didn't offer you a reset?"

"They didn't." Sloane injected all the high-pitched panic she could muster into her voice. And she could muster a good deal of it. "If I don't get in here, my uncle Morik is going to kill me. *Literally*. He *said* so. He said, 'Niece or not, if you screw up one more job, you're out.'

Except he said it all snotty and serious, and he *meant* it."

The representative didn't say anything. Sloane wondered if she'd died from shock.

"I'm sure he's a priority customer," Sloane added. "I'm just sure of it. *Please.*"

Another beat of silence. "Morik," the woman said, only the slightest tremor in her tone betraying her recognition of the name. Admirable, honestly.

"Yes," Sloane confirmed. "*That* Morik. He said if I don't do this for him, he'll attach tubes to my toes and suck all my blood out through my feet. You know who he is. Who he works for."

The woman cleared her throat. "Yes, well. Let me see what I can do. Please hold."

Sloane looked up to give Alex and Curtis a thumbs-up, but they were just staring at her, Alex's lips slightly parted.

"What?" Sloane said. "You've never called customer service?"

"You're not returning panties," Alex said. "You're in the middle of a heist."

"I wouldn't return panties," Sloane said.

The line went live again. "OK, ma'am," the woman said, "I've performed a reset on the hardware. Enter your new code when the light turns orange."

The light turned orange. Sloane entered '1 1 1 1 1.'

The light turned green.

"Oh, you've saved my life," Sloane said. "Literally."

"My pleasure," the woman said. "Tell your uncle we helped you. Please. And if you'd be willing to stay on the line to complete a brief survey about your experience today—"

"Oh, of course! Definitely, thank you *so* much."

The survey started, and Sloane ended the call. She entered the new passcode, and the door clicked open.

"Huh," Alex said.

Sloane had a microsecond to enjoy her triumph.

And then a man barreled out of the open door, slamming it back against the wall as he made his escape. The door swung back toward his face, but he was already out, running straight into Curtis. With a roar, he knocked the old man to the floor.

"Watch it," Sloane said. "He needs to pay me."

The prisoner, unfortunately, didn't seem overly concerned about her money. He hulked over Curtis for a brief second, then reeled back and punched the old man in the face. Even after the prison time, muscles ballooned from his upper arms, and his bulk was unmistakable. He had a patch of ink-black hair, and that was about all Sloane had time to take in before he started screaming.

"You lying cheat," the prisoner said. "You left me to rot in here."

"Easy, Brighton," Curtis said, his voice muffled by what had to be a rapidly swelling lip. "I'm here, ain't I? Brought help, didn't I?"

The cadence of his speech had changed. Devolved. Sloane narrowed her eyes.

Brighton, she thought, looked to be on the edge of tears. "Sixteen months, Corbin. Sixteen!"

"Couldn't be helped," Curtis said.

Brighton reared back like he was planning to hit Curtis again. But Sloane grabbed his fist. "We need to get out of here," she said.

Brighton dropped his hand, looking at her like he hadn't realized she was there. "Her?" he said.

Sloane blinked, confused. "Do I know you?"

Curtis staggered to his feet, using the door for support. "Only choice. No other takers."

Brighton frowned, but Curtis reached into the interior pocket of his atmo suit.

When he withdrew his hand, he was holding a plasma gun. Which he pointed at Sloane and Alex. See, if she'd reviewed her psychology notes, she might've seen this coming. Though come to think of it, she was pretty sure she'd skipped that class more often than not.

"Sorry about this," Curtis said. "But it had to be this way."

Sloane shook her head. "What way? You're going to shoot us?"

Curtis backed toward the airlock, Brighton at his side. "Someone always has to be on the station, or it'll explode." He made the sound, spit flying. "Discourages escape, yeah?"

"In a really stupid way," Sloane said.

"Take that up with Sever when you see him," Curtis said.

Brighton looked apologetic, but he just shrugged. Not apologetic enough to stop his friend from rescuing him at her expense, apparently.

The two men backed into the airlock, where Brighton donned an emergency atmo suit and Curtis kept the gun aimed at Sloane and Alex. They cycled the air through, and then they were gone.

Alex lifted her visor. A few rogue strands of red hair sprang loose from her bun to lick at the sides of the helmet, as if they wanted to taste the air. "I should've taken that job in the Torrent System."

"Someone offered you a job in the Torrent System?"

"People are always offering me jobs." Sloane thought the scientist was trying to be nonchalant, but Alex's gaze was darting around so quickly she couldn't possibly be registering their surroundings. She was scared. Who could blame her? Hell, Sloane was scared, too.

Who designed a station to *explode* if no one was on it?

Alex licked her lips. "So, what do we do now?"

See, this was the problem with someone else naming you the captain of their ship. Sloane wasn't a captain. She wasn't a leader. She was a mediocre med student, the daughter of a respected politician, a serial dater, and a flaky friend.

Sloane's earbud beeped, and she practically fainted in relief. Hilda. She was still nearby. Ish. Without any method of approaching, but surely the pilot would have some idea of what to do next.

The relief lasted a full second. And then Hilda spoke.

"Anyone know who's peppering *Moneymaker* with plasma shots?"

So much for a rescue squad. "Probably Curtis Corbin," Sloane said.

"The client?"

"Yeah."

Hilda cursed. "I should've known."

"It was a Federation-approved gig," Sloane said. "We couldn't have known."

Oliver might've. Sloane might be able to spot a fake handbag, but Oliver lived and breathed this world. If the stamp had been forged, he might've spotted it.

And if Sloane had spent more time learning to read

people instead of handbags, she might've spotted Oliver's fraud. Curtis's, too.

"Guess Curtis had a ship after all," Alex said.

Obviously he had a ship. Who was flying it, and where they'd been hiding, Sloane couldn't say.

Hilda cursed again. "Shields are not going to hold for long here. I'll try to chase them away. Can you two escape?"

"Not without getting shrapnel in our asses," Sloane said. "Try to stick nearby."

"Might be in a million pieces, but I'll do my best."

Sloane squinted down the hall, then paced to the airlock where Curtis and Brighton had ditched them. She pressed her hands to the window and peered out, as if she could see the *Moneymaker* through the airlock and the enemy that was trying to blow it to bits. She went over the layout of the station in her mind, cataloging the features she'd seen from outside.

She hadn't been paying enough attention. But she'd been paying some.

"Sever wasn't stupid," she said.

"The person who talks about him in past tense might be," Alex replied.

"Alex, did this station have plasma cannons? Rail guns?"

"I counted four on the way in."

Trust Alex to pay attention. "Do you think you could find the plasma chambers?"

"I'm afraid to ask why."

Sloane backed away from the door. This place smelled like rust and mold, and she was not going to stay here. "Because Curtis's supposed explosion wouldn't do any good with the shields up."

"How do you figure?"

"The shields would contain the blast, which would protect the person who just escaped without a ship nearby."

"But the shields *aren't* up."

"So we activate them."

Alex threw her hands up, but the bulk of her suit stole most of the power of the gesture. "Then how do we get out of here? The matter-phaser is dead."

Sloane licked her lips. "I can think of one path that leads straight out of the station."

Alex stared at her. Hard. "Do not say what I think you're going to say."

Sloane clapped the scientist on the shoulder. No point in delaying the inevitable. "Do you think we'd fit inside a plasma cannon?"

IT ONLY MADE SENSE.

The station wouldn't explode with the shields up, so they needed to get the shields up. And escape before the rail guns could start shooting. No problem.

For the first time, Sloane's ignorance about space stuff was starting to pay off. Her crew could roll their eyes at her all they wanted, but facts were facts. Alex had gotten them in, but Sloane would get them out. And she'd do it her way.

It wasn't hard to find the plasma gun room. Deck. Whatever. Sloane didn't know the technical term, and there wasn't a sign above the door.

There *were* twelve sea-green tanks, each about ten

meters tall, with ladders strung up the sides for anyone who wanted to risk their lives for reasons unknown.

Or, Sloane assumed, to refill the tanks with brand new loads of plasma. Nice and shiny. And deadly.

Sloane stepped around the tanks and pointed to the square divots up on the wall. Plasma-loading chambers, which led into the plasma cannon barrels, which led, presumably, into the depths of space. The rest of the room was full of panels and chains and gears and whatever else — mechanisms to move the rail guns, maybe, or change plasma tanks. She doubted people tended to do this by hand.

But they *could*. With a wrench in the right place, or a loosened screw, the guns would fail.

"Step one," Sloane said, "disable the rail guns."

Alex looked at her. Blinked three times. Confused, maybe. So Sloane pointed to the tanks, the mechanisms, the *stuff* that appeared to make the cannons shoot at things.

"What, you want *me* to do that?"

Sloane nodded.

Alex rubbed a hand across her face. "I don't know how many times I need to tell you that I'm not a mechanic or a weapons expert. I'm an *astrophysicist*."

Conversely, Sloane didn't know how many inventions Alex would have to work up — in the name of 'hobbies' — before she realized she *was* good at all this cord-button-beeping-machine stuff. "Just do your best."

Alex sucked in her cheeks, then winced as if she'd bitten herself particularly hard. "If the systems are connected and I disable the rail guns, the explosives might be triggered. Especially if the shield isn't activated yet."

Geniuses always had to be so pragmatic.

"All right then," Sloane said. "Step one is to crawl through the plasma cannons."

Without waiting for a response, she climbed the tank wall, crawled across the top, and dropped into the open chamber where plasma would presumably flow from the tank to the cannon before blasting out to wipe a ship into oblivion.

"You're going to get us killed," Alex said.

"Feel free to live a nice life in this prison. Brighton seemed well-fed, so I'm sure you'd survive."

"I would," Alex said. "I really would. Except for the fact that you're going to get this place blown up, anyway."

"Not if you stay."

Alex started to climb.

Already sweating, Sloane waited for Alex to join her before pulling herself into the barrel of the cannon. From a distance, these things always looked huge. She'd pictured herself sitting inside the circle at the end, legs dangling — already a fallacy in zero gravity — waiting comfortably for her ride.

Now that she was inside, the walls closed in around her like a snake ready to squeeze. Her gloves scraped along the bottom, and she practically had to pull herself along.

She hoped it wouldn't get any narrower.

"OK," Sloane said, breathing hard. "Step two: get Hilda to fly close and activate the shields."

She nearly stopped moving as she instructed the communication link to ping Hilda — was it getting hotter in here? — but Alex punched the bottom of her foot to keep her moving.

"Hilda," Sloane said, "can you get close to the station?"

"Negative. Kind of busy over here."

Sloane could hear the frantic screaming of alarms in the background, the rumble of *Moneymaker*'s engine trying to keep from imploding.

She couldn't help Hilda.

She could only help herself. And Alex.

Arms shaking from the effort of pulling herself forward, Sloane told her helmet to redial the last number she'd called before Hilda.

"Property Protect Limited mechanism department, how can I help you?"

She'd been hoping for a different representative, but it was definitely the same syrupy-sweet woman from before. Because of course it was. "Hi," Sloane said, "it's me again. Morik's niece?"

A beat. "Ma'am," the representative said, "this is highly irregular."

Sloane could see the stars twinkling beyond the mouth of the cannon now, the rainbow ebb of the closest current path in the distance. She was close now. So close.

"You don't know the half of it," she said. "Listen, I was lying before. I'm actually trying to break someone out of prison at this station. You should probably call the Fleet."

Silence. "What was that, ma'am?"

"I'm on the station, I'm stealing shit, I'm about to escape. Sever's going to blame you, probably. Send the Fleet. Thanks so much!"

Sloane ended the call.

"That is not going to work," Alex said. "We're going to die."

"We are not."

"All right, then what's step three?"

Step three: dive out of the gun, get onto the ship, and fly away. In the six seconds it would take the plasma to load.

Yeah, OK, they were probably going to die.

Sloane inched to the edge of the cannon, the lip now within her grasp. She pulled her body halfway out, scraping the rocket booster on the barrel above her as she did. She hoped to the stars it would still function.

The woman had to call the Fleet. She had to turn them in.

She had to.

Panicked breaths fogged Sloane's visor, coming too fast and hot for the environment system to scoop up the moisture. Maybe the woman *had* called. Maybe the Fleet didn't care.

But the Fleet was a stuck-up club full of self-right-eous, power-hungry bureaucrats. There was no way they'd miss an opportunity like this.

As the thought crossed her mind, the current spat out a gray-sided Fleet Cruiser, its orange stripes clashing with the bright blue shield that pulsed around the ship.

She could have kissed it, ugly hull and all.

"Grab my ankles," Sloane said.

Alex did, and Sloane pushed herself free of the station as the ship sailed through the shields, rocketing them both toward the oncoming cruiser.

Sloane had always felt that Fleet officers were stuffy.

The Fleet officers sitting around the table in their stuffy boardroom on their stuffy warship had sticks lodged even further up than most. They all wore identically short haircuts and watched her with identically disapproving stares.

And she hadn't even criticized their orange stripes.

"Ms. Tarnish," the captain said — because this was a captain-worthy moment that had pulled him away from his Very Important work on the bridge. "You just released a Level 14 criminal into the galaxy. Explain yourself."

Sloane didn't know for sure if Level 14 meant he was really bad, or if he'd dined and dashed a few times. All the same in the Fleet's eyes, anyway.

"It was a Federation-approved bounty," she said, for what felt like the fifty-millionth time and was probably the hundred-millionth time. "Stamped and everything. If you need to prosecute someone, prosecute them for letting it slip by. Maybe it was a mole."

Or a hack, or just a really good fake. Even the mighty Cosmic Trade Federation made mistakes from time to time.

"Besides," Alex said placidly, "the prisoner was being held by Sever. We figured that meant it really was a rescue."

Sloane gave her a thumbs-up. Good point, Alex. Good point.

Another officer cleared his throat. "Their pilot did send the files. The other ship fled as soon as we arrived."

And thank goodness for that. Hilda was fine. She'd survived. Sloane wanted to cry in relief.

But not in front of these guys.

"The stamp was real," the officer added.

"Someone got into the system," another said.

"Or they've been compromised." Yet another.

Sloane wouldn't be surprised if these guys stormed

out to raid the Federation right this minute. Not that they'd win. But they'd certainly feel good about themselves right up until the moment the Federation ground their ship into dust.

The captain held up a hand. "We'll reach out to the CTF. Right after we figure out what to do with Ms. Tarnish and her associates."

Worst band name ever. "So, if I understand this right, you had Sever imprisoning a Level 14 prisoner for you? Don't you have your own facilities?"

She only hoped she wouldn't be headed for one.

The captain rubbed his chin. "Not exactly *for* us." He said it like a confession.

One point to him for not lying, she supposed. That didn't mean she was letting him off the hook, though. "So this criminal guy got on Sever's bad side, and you just . . . let him stay there?" Sloane tsked. "That's bad form, captain."

To the captain's credit, he didn't say anything about the decision being above his pay grade. Though it probably would've been. He sighed. "Your schooner is docking. You're free to go. Perhaps to choose a different trade."

Sloane got up and mocked a curtsy. "Thanks for the rescue, friends."

Alex rolled her eyes and headed out the door. Probably missing her bunny slippers. Though Sloane hoped she'd turn her attention to more matter-phasing type inventions. Sloane moved to follow. She hoped the shower cyclers hadn't been re-damaged in Hilda's battle.

"Ms. Tarnish?"

Sloane turned when the captain spoke, one hand on the door frame.

"We have reason to believe Sever is gone for good," the captain said. "Adu System is going to see a power vacuum. I suggest you steer clear."

"I will," Sloane said.

At least, she would if she could. And if not, well, Sloane had never had a problem making promises she couldn't keep.

Sloane and her friends star in Kate Sheeran Swed's Parse Galaxy series, as well as having a cameo in her League of Independent Operatives superhero series, where they show up in Book 2.

Get a free sci-fi short story collection and VIP library access at www.katesheeranswed.com/free-books.

HOT MEAL
BY MARK NIEMANN-ROSS

DETECTIVE ARACI BELO ADMIRES THE VIEW OF POST-earthquake Portland from this small condominium. The west hills provide a lush green background to the dense housing towers, interconnected by skyways and hyper-tube stations.

He considers the shattered condo he stands in. The explosion had propelled bits of the oven from the back of the condo, spraying shrapnel towards the window. A sweet, meaty smell of burnt flesh emanates from Dakota Williams, the recently deceased occupant. She lies in the middle of the room, her severed right arm near the earth-quake pillar. Her left forearm leans against the wall. The explosion burned through her clothing, face, and skin.

Pieces of meal boxes are scattered around. How many is difficult to know; metal and plastic shards are mixed with uncooked food. One is in the far corner, complete except for a dented top. The cube, small enough to hold in both hands, is covered with a bright depiction of the traditional (soy-based) steak and potatoes with Brussels sprouts.

Araci steps around Dakota and through the door to the other half of the condominium containing a bedroom and bath. The bathroom is tidy, but not spotless. There are two toothbrushes in a cup and enough towels for a couple. The bedroom has a desk cluttered with electronic parts. The bed is neat; the floor picked up except for a few kitchen utensils thrown in by the explosion.

"The scan is ready," says Officer Guadalupe Reyes, one of the many people swarming the condominium. She pushes a button on a hand-held terminal. "I've put the render in the report folder. You interested in grabbing some dinner tonight?"

Guadalupe — sometimes "Lupe" — is Araci's sparring partner in the Portland Police self-defense class. Their relationship is professional, although there are signals something more might be possible.

"Sure. Six pm?" replies Araci. "Come to my place and I'll make you a meal that doesn't explode."

"You are such a buzzkill. I was hoping for excitement." She grabs her bags and pushes through the crowd. "See you tonight."

Araci reviews the scan in his visor and compares two overlaid views; the real, burned room, and the original as shown in the floorplan. An augmented reality outline fills in the missing parts of the destroyed oven. It was a countertop unit, and all that remains is the back panel and fuel tank. Everything splayed outwards from where the oven used to be; the explosion had clearly occurred there.

Araci retrieves the steak and potatoes meal from the corner of the main room and wonders if it's broken. He can't afford one of the expensive Hestia ovens; instead, he boils food packets like every other middle-class American. Araci turns the meal box over, shakes it, puts it down.

Normally, Hestia food boxes and ovens produce a perfect dinner. This time, Hestia took an angry turn for the worse.

Lupe's scan allows for an animated reconstruction of the explosion, tracing the path of the scattered parts back to their original assembly. Araci plays it forward and reverse three times. What happened is clear: Dakota had been standing in front of the oven when it exploded and distributed a high-velocity cloud of sharp plastic, metal, and glass through her and into the room.

As for this condo, there was nothing more. He ships the report to the Portland Police server and leaves the apartment clean-up to the forensics team.

Araci Belo loves being a police detective. He looks young for a middle-aged guy; Lupe stands near the kitchen counter with a glass of wine, watching him fuss with the presentation.

Araci assembles Chicken Piccata, one of the more complex meals available in pouches. He enjoys cooking, the reveal of ingredients from each foil bag, the simple preparation, the assembly. He isn't dedicated enough to work from raw foods; pre-measured packets are his limit. The *smell* of onions when they emerge from the sauté packet. Squeezing lemon slices on the chicken. Sprinkling capers, salt, and pepper just before plating.

Building a meal from scratch would be even better, but grocery stores removed their coolers and freezers long ago. The logistics of a foil packet are much simpler than transporting fresh vegetables or meat.

"You should buy one of those ovens," observes Lupe.

"You like cooking. You could make more complex meals."

"I considered it, but after today, I'm not so sure." Araci moves the two plates to the table, refills both wine glasses, and invites Lupe. "I've seen the advertisements. Push the meal box into the oven and stand back. Where's the romance?"

"Maybe not romance, but how would you print a steak without one?"

"Print steak how?" asks Araci. "You can't do that at home."

"Right. Not with a packet boiler," says Lupe. "That's the big deal with a Hestia oven. When you insert a meal into the oven, it engages with electricity, a data port, and a gas port. The gas flows into chambers in the meal box. The meal box controls the addition of ingredients and supervises printing any meat. The oven connects the meal to the outside world. The entire setup is patented."

"So there's a meat printer in the meal box?"

"I know! It doesn't seem like there's enough room. But the meal opens a valve, meat paste pours out, the oven cooks it, another layer of meat paste, some flavors, more cooking. Pretty soon you have a New York steak. Can't do that with foil packets."

"I did not know," admits Araci. He looks suspiciously at the chicken on his fork. "But here's a question; why gas? Why not just heat with electricity?"

"Good question," replies Lupe. "Hestia can't charge for electricity, but they can sell you overpriced gas canisters. You can't refill a Hestia tank, you have to buy a new one. Like ink for printers: Buy it from the manufacturer or they won't work."

"I get it," says Araci. He accepts the chicken for what it is and takes another bite. "Are you up for ice cream? I bought a tube of cherry chunk."

ARACI'S DAY starts with a call to Hestia, the center of suspicion. His call is met with an artificially intelligent receptionist, projected through his visor as though sitting across from him at the desk.

"Hello, Araci Belo," says the receptionist. It wasn't surprising they knew his name; he was easy to identify from his online presence. "I'm here to help." The AI exhibits artificial signs of life: her eyes blink, she breathes. But she waits, saying nothing more.

"I'd like to speak to the Hestia oven Product Manager," replies Araci.

The receptionist doesn't hesitate. "I'm sorry, but our product managers are only available by appointment. Can I connect you with our media spokesperson?"

"No. I'm with the Portland Police Department, and I'm working on a case involving your Hestia ovens." Araci enunciates and speaks slowly, emphasizing the word 'Police.'

"One minute, please." the receptionist pauses, then fades to black. In their place appears a dark-haired, middle-aged man. He looks up and adjusts something on his desk.

"Hello, Mr. Belo. My name is Farj Capcin. I'm the Product Manager for Hestia ovens. I'm told you have some questions." He waves his hand from off-screen to the center of his view, adding two more individuals. "This is

Ms. Broin, our attorney, and Mr. Nilsson, who manages media relations. Since you are a police representative, we are recording this call. Do you object?"

"Feel free." The prickly reception did not surprise Araci. He'd used his detective status to get the receptionist to act, but knew it would put everyone on guard.

"I'm investigating the death of Dakota Williams . . ."

Araci hasn't finished speaking, but Broin, the attorney, immediately searches for something. She taps Farj and points to whatever she found. Farj mutes and gestures to Broin. Nilsson leans in to look at Broin's display, rubs his balding head, and speaks to Farj. He turns to Nilsson, then Broin, confers for a minute, then returns to Araci.

"Dakota Williams is a member of Abundancy. We support the idea of unrestricted food for all and have issued several statements regarding our eagerness to accomplish this within the bounds of our corporation's abilities."

Farj recites this without hesitation. This is not the first time he has addressed issues with the Abundancy group. Araci wonders if the AI receptionist knows the line as well.

Araci isn't familiar with Abundancy. Pretending to make a note, he opens a search. He quickly learns Abundancy is an activist group; part Greenpeace, part Free Software Foundation, part Earth First, part Right to Repair. They accuse Hestia of trying to patent food, similar to how DuPont and Monsanto hold patents on genetically modified corn, soybean, and alfalfa. Abundancy argues Hestia will eventually claim rights to any method of combining food to make a meal.

Abundancy has protested. They haven't gone as far as

breaking windows at Hestia factories, but they have disrupted shareholder meetings and sent letters just shy of threatening bodily harm. Abundancy lists Dakota as a volunteer, but the search doesn't describe her responsibilities.

Wasn't it strange for Dakota to own a device from the Great Satan Hestia? thinks Araci.

He returns to the conversation. "I'm more interested in an explosion of one of your devices."

Farj again mutes and confers, then answers Araci. "We know Ms. Williams owns a Hestia oven, but that unit has not responded to our status requests for several weeks. She has refused to allow us to provide maintenance, so we aren't liable."

"What have you heard about the malfunction?" asks Araci. "Have you determined the cause?"

"We had a team onsite, and I'm able to supply you with their report," says Farj. "I suspect you found the same; the oven wasn't intact, and it was difficult to recover the pieces."

"So you don't know what happened?"

"Correct," answers Farj. "When we do, we'll be happy to share those findings."

Araci ends the call. Hestia won't provide any more information, so it makes little sense to keep asking. He'll need more details before speaking with them again.

Onwards to his next call.

"Hello, I'm Araci Belo," he says. The AI fielding calls for Abundancy isn't impressed; it might even be broken. It is a virtual puppet projected into his room, only showing a gray outline of a humanoid. There is no face, and the normal signs of life are missing.

"I'm investigating the death of Dakota Williams," Araci says.

Nothing.

"I can get a search warrant if necessary," tries Araci. "I can have you audited and put your non-profit status on hold."

The gray humanoid abruptly gains nuances of life. Its head tracks Araci's movement; its left hand fidgets. The right moves an unseen control. It speaks.

"Detective Araci, we're not stupid. Please don't threaten us with legal action you can't follow up on," says whoever is behind the puppet. "However, since you're investigating what happened to Dakota, I want to make certain you're aware of all the facts."

"I recently spoke to Hestia," states Araci. "They mentioned your organization."

"I'm sure they did. Hestia is trying to restrict access to food. They built their oven to work with their food — and *only* their food. They control the seed, they control the harvest, they control the preparation. It's proprietary from field to consumer, locking out anyone who wants to do it themselves. That's wrong, and Abundancy is working to prevent it."

"But Hestia only controls food boxes and ovens," says Araci. "They aren't stopping me from using a boiler and a pouch."

"Not yet. But boil pouches made fresh food obsolete. Hestia will eventually try to make boiler pouches obsolete. Then yes, they will stop you from cooking with boiler and pouch."

"That's interesting, but I'm mainly concerned about Dakota. What was she working on?"

"Dakota was working on her own time and had an

interest in the mechanics of the oven and meal boxes. I suggest you look at the financial impact to Hestia if they were to lose control of their food system. It might be worth killing someone. Not that corporations have ever done anything evil."

"I appreciate your theories. When you're ready to speak face to face, please contact me." Araci ends the call.

Would a corporation kill to protect intellectual property? Of course they would.

Araci's visor announces a request from Lupe, which he gladly accepts. "Araci, we're finding some interesting details in the scan of the condominium explosion. It takes some high resolution, come over to the media lab and see."

THE POLICE MEDIA lab isn't much more than a room with desks and monitors. The striking feature is the glass wall with a view of the servers. Privacy laws require this type of data to be under actual lock and key, so Araci has to visit in person.

"We had the render machines spend some quality time with the scans and found this interesting difference." Lupe displays the condominium scan Araci viewed earlier but in much higher resolution.

"There are two things you should see," says Lupe. "Let's start with the oven reconstruction."

Lupe waves the condo into view, then spreads her hands to enlarge the space where the oven used to be. Spinning her fingers counterclockwise re-assembles it to its assumed state before the explosion. To the side were two new objects: a circuit board and a meal box.

"Okay, look at this." Lupe points at the back of the

oven. "The scan couldn't find any pieces of the oven circuit board, so it left that space empty. But look at this circuit to the side — the scan found parts of it all over the room. It was near — or inside — the oven when it exploded. This isn't the standard Hestia circuit board. Someone installed a home-built version."

"Can you move to the desk?" asks Araci.

The view steps back from the oven, turns, and glides to the bedroom. When Araci had physically been there, he had seen electronics. They are visible in the render currently being shown, with the addition of tags identifying the parts.

Many of the tags identify stock electronics. The largest circuit is a Hestia board belonging to the oven in the other room. Lupe points it out. "Dakota took this out of the Hestia and installed a home-built version."

"So Dakota wasn't using the oven for food. She was doing research. That's one mystery partially solved," says Araci. "You mentioned you had two interesting things to show me?"

"Yes." She moves the view to the meal box. It's in bad shape, with large, jagged gaps.

"Look. Right here," says Lupe. "This serial number on the meal is partially damaged. But it doesn't correspond to anything available on the open market. We don't know where she got it."

"A mystery meal in an altered oven," says Araci. "Operator error compounded by hackery?"

"Did you find the missing roommate?" asks Lupe. "Toothbrushes? Towels?"

"I haven't had time to search Dakota's timeline in depth. How about now?" Araci taps his visor and speaks a command. "Display Dakota Williams social history."

Snippets from Dakota's life appear in Araci's visor; he shares them with Lupe. In a video dated January 2059, a man named Robin Lopez first appears. The videos of Dakota and Robin become playful, then intimate, leading up to their move to the condo.

A quick search for Robin Lopez shows he also works for Abundancy. He is the author of 'The Road to Food Free from Restrictions,' and Hestia is his nemesis.

"So if they were both with Abundancy and fighting with Hestia, why did they have one of the ovens? Maybe Hestia didn't like what she was doing?" suggests Lupe. "They have all sorts of control over that thing. Can they tell it to explode?"

"Or... maybe Robin didn't like something Dakota was doing?" adds Araci. "I wonder where he is?"

ARACI's last task of the day is to speak with Dakota's next of kin. Of course, Dakota's family has already heard about her death. It's impossible for Araci to be the point of first contact when everything is public to everyone. But visiting the family is the most human part of his job — and the most difficult.

Dakota's father lives in a studio apartment. Neighbor kids play on the balcony overlooking the urban canyon formed by buildings and streets below. Araci knocks and is greeted by an older man dressed in a light shirt and shorts. "You must be Detective Belo," he says. "I'm Archer Williams. Dakota's father. Please come in."

"I'm sorry to tell you about your daughter's death," replies Araci. "She died from an explosion in her home."

"I know, and I thank you for your concern. Can I offer

you a drink?" Archer mixes powder in water. It fizzes, and Araci smells red wine. He accepts the glass and takes a sip to demonstrate his solidarity with Archer.

"To Dakota," says Archer.

"To your daughter," responds Araci. "Again, I'm sorry." A moment of respectful silence passes before he speaks again.

"We're investigating the explosion now. Is there anything we can tell you — or that you would like us to know?"

"Yes, there is." Archer puts down the glass and crosses his arms. "Dakota was a good engineer. Not brilliant, but decent enough to accomplish what she needed to do. School wasn't easy for her. She had to struggle to finish that degree. But it taught her to be careful, persistent, and not to assume her initial instinct was correct." Archer chokes up, wipes his eyes. He takes a breath and continues, "That's why I'm surprised she got caught in an explosion. She never expected things would run the first or second time, so she planned for failure."

"I assume you know she was experimenting with the oven?"

"I don't know all the details. She didn't want me to know what she was doing for Abundancy. That is a strange group. Actually, it is a strange boy. I'm certain Abundancy isn't anything more than Robin Lopez."

"I'm looking for Robin. I believe he was living with Dakota. But he's disappeared."

"That doesn't surprise me." Archer picks up the wine and swirls the glass. "Lopez does what he needs to get what he wants. Dakota had a stable job, and she enjoyed it. Lopez convinced her to work on his Abundancy project instead. Dakota was careful, unless she was with Lopez. Then she moved fast and broke things. Lopez is impulsive, reckless, and coercive. None of those are good qualities."

"Mr. Williams, if you hear from Robin Lopez, would you tell me?" asks Araci. "And if there is anything else you'd like to learn from me, I'm at your service."

The sun is setting over the adjoining building when Araci leaves Archer Williams' apartment. With a trace more dust in the air, it might look like a wilderness landscape.

ARACI GREETS the morning with instant coffee. Normally he boils a pouch of pre-brewed, but today he has things to do. Powder, hot water, drink. Araci opens a call to Hestia. After wrangling with the AI receptionist, Farj Capcin appears.

"I have a few details I'd like to show you, but you'll want to do this in person," says Araci. "If you were to get a seat on the hyperloop, you could be here in time for an afternoon conference. Yes?"

"Normally no," replies Farj. "But I have a light day, and I'm intrigued. Are you buying lunch?"

"Sure. I'll meet you at the counter in the PDX downtown station."

ARACI PAYS for lunch with Farj and Nilsson, the marketing guy for Hestia. They catch the light rail to the police media station where Lupe already has the render of the oven displayed and two boxes to the side.

"We've done some forensics and need your ideas on what we've discovered," explains Araci.

"Do you mind if I explore?" asks Farj. Lupe gives him control, and he rushes to examine the circuit board. "I don't suppose you have the actual parts?"

"No, but we have something we think is related." Araci opens the first box, displaying the electronics from Dakota's desk. "Dakota was working on this, but we're not sure what it is. We're hoping you have some insight."

Farj picks up the box and adjusts his visor, peering at the parts with high magnification. After a minute, Farj turns to Nilsson and makes a brief comment.

"It's obvious Dakota was attempting to violate our intellectual property and patents," Farj says to Lupe and Araci. "Much of this is stock components. We do it differently, but the logic is likely the same."

Araci redirects the conversation. "Let's look at this other box."

Araci hands it to Farj; it contains what is left of the meal boxes. "These aren't available on the market. I'm guessing it's something you are working on and somehow Dakota got a sample."

Nilsson seemed puzzled, but Farj was alarmed. He leans in and examines pieces of the exploded meal parts, taking pictures of each. Putting down the box, he adjusts his visor for several minutes.

Farj sits back. "I'll explain later," he tells Nilsson. Nilsson rubs his head and starts to object, but Farj cuts him off.

"I really can't talk about this," Farj tells Araci.

"Is it something you built? Did Dakota build it?" Araci tries to get an answer from Farj.

"No. I can't discuss this without a lawyer present." Farj abruptly stands and motions for Nilsson to do the same. "We need to catch the loop home."

Araci knows there are plenty of hyperloops back to San Francisco. Farj is making an excuse to leave. Something about the meal has him on edge. They barely have time to end the meeting before Farj and Nilsson are out the door and gone.

"What was that?" asks Lupe.

"A tell," replies Araci. "A clue. Maybe Abundancy has some ideas. And I have a hunch . . ."

Araci opens a call on his visor and shares it with Lupe. The same gray puppet appears.

"Um...Dakota Williams, search warrant, audit, non-profit," says Araci. If he's lucky, the AI will respond to those keywords. The puppet pauses, then twitches under human control.

"Detective Belo, what is it now?" The puppet performs an adequate simulation of annoyance.

"We have a question about a meal kit, as well as electronics Dakota put in the oven."

"I — Abundancy — wouldn't know anything about that," says the puppet.

"I'd also like to speak with Robin Lopez," says Araci. "I believe that would be you."

The puppet freezes. "I don't . . . Robin isn't . . ."

"I can get a privacy exemption if necessary," says Araci. "So, Robin, shall we be real?"

The puppet looks away, then reshapes its features. Araci recognizes this new face as Robin from Dakota's videos.

"We wondered where you were," says Araci. "Hiding after someone dies is suspicious — wouldn't you agree?"

"I'm trying to stay alive," says Robin. "The explosion was not an accident. I stepped out to get us something to eat and when I returned, there were alarms and smoke. Dakota was dead, and whoever caused the explosion might have still been around. I took a quick look, then ran."

"Okay. You got scared and ran. Let's accept that for now. But Dakota had installed a custom circuit board in the oven. Maybe an accident, but suppose you two brought this on yourselves."

"NO. We did not." Robin chokes up. "Dakota was smart. And careful."

"What was Dakota trying to do with this circuit?" Araci asks.

"It's not that remarkable — her modification intercepts and logs commands from the meal. We were recording the cooking process. With enough information, we could build open-source meals. Hestia is tricky about how they make the system work — we were going to free that up to the world. That's why they killed Dakota."

"That seems extreme," starts Araci. "But where did that meal come from? Would I be able to purchase that from a grocery vendor?"

Robin hesitates. "Not yet." He looks away for a minute, sighs, and looks back. "They aren't commercially available. Friends of ours *found it* on a shipping dock."

"So, you stole an experimental meal, then stuffed it in a modified oven," says Araci "That wasn't a smart thing to do."

"Hestia already tested it — they were ready to release.

They somehow interfered with our experiment and set off a bomb. Dakota and I didn't know that was possible, or we wouldn't have been doing that."

"So, you want me to believe Hestia reached out from the void and triggered an explosion?"

"Is that so hard to accept? They have access to everything. They can upgrade the oven software. They can shut it off. Why wouldn't they aggressively defend their competitive advantage?"

"You said you were getting something to eat. But Dakota was cooking a meal."

"Dakota was testing how the meal worked, not to eat it. Most of the time, the cooking process didn't work, and the food was inedible. We could see the meal communicate with the oven with earlier test, but Dakota's circuit just logged the request. The meal assumed everything was fine. Most of it came out like old soybeans and congealed fat. Nasty stuff."

AT HOME, Araci is moving chairs for the robot vacuum when his visor announces a call. It's someone using a privacy puppet.

"Hello, Robin," answers Araci. "Is there something new you'd like to discuss?"

"This isn't Robin," says the puppet. "I want to help you review your assumptions about Dakota Williams and Robin Lopez."

Whoever is driving this animation has access to luxurious bandwidth. Robin's puppet had been featureless. In comparison, this is a middle-aged woman with astonishing

detail in her face. Her hair is layered in an intricate simulation of a bob cut. Puppets are sometimes only rendered
from the waist up; this is a full-body complete with
sensible shoes.

"Well, I've got a lot of important things to do today."
Araci considers the vacuum cleaner. "But I'm always
interested in a mystery. Please continue."

"You need to consider the meal Dakota was playing
with," she says. "Unfortunately, there isn't enough of it
left for you to examine. If you don't already know, you
can't buy them. Yet. Dakota's accident only added a
round of testing. It will not make a difference. They're
dangerous."

She continues, "The meals are difficult to understand.
You would have to hire some high-powered electrical
engineers and some equally high-powered food engineers,
then do months of research to figure out what's unusual
about it."

Araci sends the robot off to the other room. "You're
making a lot of claims, and you tell me I don't have the
wattage to check your conclusions. I'll state the obvious:
why should I trust you?"

"Because I work for Hestia," says the woman. She
rubs her head in an un-feminine way, scrambling her neat
hairstyle. "These new meals are going to get us in trouble,
but I'm unable to convince anyone we should stop the
project. Your investigation will make an impression."

The woman holds up a meal box. "I've sent you one
of these. When you get it, you'll be able to prove what I'm
about to show you." The box doubles in size, then changes
to a cutaway view showing a starburst pattern of food
cavities, channels, pumps, valves, and electronics. A chip
throbs with a blue outline.

"This chip, the one outlined in blue, is a new concept for meals. It's full-blown artificial intelligence. It doesn't make the meal sing or dance. It just solves problems — like any other AI. But it does two special things. First, it confirms the food preparation process is going according to plan. If not, it adjusts the recipe to recover. Second, it sends that learning to our server."

Araci sits down. The woman puppet takes a step closer and also sits, a chair materializing under her. A perfectly smooth animation; Araci forgot he was talking to thin air.

"I assume all Hestia meals communicate with the network," says Araci.

"True. But we only collect what's legal. Privacy laws restrict what can be recorded. This new meal dodges that restriction. It doesn't record the actions of the user; it records the actions of the AI. The AI responds to the oven and the user. See the difference?"

"That's a slim distinction. Something a judge would be interested in discussing."

"Try Congress and legislation," she says. "This is a game-changer and not just for food."

"Sounds like a job for a lobbyist. But back to what matters. I'm interested in what — or who — blew up Dakota."

The puppet drops the meal, and it vanishes. "It's the AI. We can't test it because we don't have Dakota's circuit, and the telemetry from the meal is confused. We're certain the AI tried to control things. The oven didn't respond predictably, so the AI improvised. Somehow the AI decided it needed to open the gas valve. But the valve was already open. Dakota's circuit gave the AI inaccurate information."

"The meal allowed the tank to discharge the entire volume of gas. But the AI made a mistake, and it sparked an igniter. If we release these meals without understanding the risks, consumers won't trust Hestia or any of their products, let alone the ovens."

"Maybe Dakota wasn't wrong," says Araci. "She may have been doing something unexpected, but that's the nature of people. If your product doesn't like that, maybe you ought to check your design?"

"You and I agree on that," she says.

"*IRASSHAIMASE!*"

Lupe and Araci enter the restaurant, and video screens scattered around the bar show a cartoon sushi chef cheerfully welcoming them for dinner. They sit at an open table. Four segments of a donut-shaped platform in the center of their table drop out of sight, one at a time, then rise up bearing drinks or food.

Araci retrieves a beer, Lupe an old-fashioned; the empty squares drop, then return with a bowl of peanuts and a salad. A robotic chef at the side of the room whirs, mixing drinks and chopping food. It's programmed to present Araci and Lupe with the most profitable menu.

"So. Whodunit?" asks Araci. "Robin thinks it was the friendly folks at Hestia. My mystery caller from Hestia thinks Dakota precipitated a fatal accident."

Lupe squeezes the orange in her drink, bites off the fruit, then drops the peel in the garbage hole in the middle of the table. A slight vacuum pulls it away. "What if Robin did it? He was suspiciously absent."

"He might have had the opportunity, but why?

Dakota and Robin were on the same team, both for Abundancy and in a relationship."

"I'll agree. But I think nothing Dakota did was enough to light things up. Seems like her circuit was fail-safe. If something didn't seem right, her circuit would just log the request."

Araci picks up the peanuts, then moves to put them back down. Too late; they are charged to his tab, and the platform drops away, reappearing with a crudité platter. He surrenders and shells a peanut. "That leaves us with Hestia, or an unfortunate accident. But I'm not convinced Farj is a killer."

"Maybe you need to focus on Robin." Lupe shows an affectionate smile. "Or maybe you should have another beer and tell me more about your interesting past life."

THE MEAL BOX was waiting at Araci's mail drop when he got home. Wrapped as a consumer package and with no return address, Araci has a justifiable concern as he brings it inside. Will Hestia make this explode as well?

When he awakes the next morning, the box is sitting exactly where he placed it. There is no evidence it has moved around during the night, or that it has released gas into the apartment. He needs to get this thing out of his life.

Araci calls Abundancy; Robin answers immediately.

"I'm going to need some help testing some crazy theories," says Araci. "You've got the knowledge to understand the internals of this problem, and you might be interested in the corporate side."

Robin — who is no longer using a puppet — checks

something off-screen. "I have access to a Hestia oven and a copy of the board Dakota was playing with. Is that the sort of setup you're looking for?"

"Close enough," replies Araci. "Let's meet. I'll bring a meal."

ARACI SUMMONS a public car and directs it to the location Robin mentioned; an artist's building, four floors of small studios all wrapped up in one big fire hazard. He knocks on the door of room 327 and meets Robin face-to-face for the first time.

"I brought dinner," says Araci. He holds out the meal sent by his anonymous lady friend.

"How convenient," replies Robin. "I've got an oven."

Robin ushers Araci into an open room with no windows. Steel columns brace the walls in a minimally legal attempt to be earthquake-proof. A workbench stretches across one wall, covered with electronic test gear. In the center is an oven with wire — actual wires — running from the oven to the diagnostic machines.

"I'm going to assume this is all legal and code-compliant," says Araci. "At least, I won't ask, so please don't tell."

Robin looks at him but reveals nothing. He powers up the oven and the displays on the workbench. They reflected frantic communication coming from the oven, but Araci cannot decipher what it means.

"What are we testing?" asks Robin.

"One of my new friends called," says Araci. "They said the meal has an AI chip that didn't enjoy talking to Dakota's custom board. They consider the explosion a miscommunication."

"We didn't even think there might be AI in the meal. That's serious engineering, way more than we gave Hestia credit for. Let's look."

"Whoa — before you connect this up, are we going to die in an unplanned fire?" Araci holds back. "I'd like to avoid that."

Robin points at a display on the bench. "I've simulated the gas tank. The meal should be happier about the oven response."

Araci surrenders the meal to Robin and takes a precautionary step backward from the project. Robin places the meal inside the oven.

The previously frantic displays become a blur. Robin goes to the workbench, taps a control once, then twice. The display converts to a summary and shows an overview of the oven's activities.

"Oh — look at that!" Robin watches an exhibit of flashing boxes and lines. He looks at Araci, realizing a better explanation was necessary. "It's the meal talking to the oven. There's so much more than Dakota expected. The AI explains a lot when you recognize it."

Araci can only guess at the story Robin is watching. Three displays jitter with confusing diagnostics; Robin bounces from one station on the workbench to another.

Abruptly, one screen freezes. Another changes its layout. The third continues but at one-half the speed. Robin looks at the oven. "What are you doing?" he asks. Not to Araci — to the oven.

Robin slaps a large red button straight out of a comic book. The workbench and oven abruptly shut down. He turns to face Araci.

"This was not an accident," says Robin. He hesitates, then paces, checking inactive displays and tracing wires.

"The meal just tried to start a fire. Not just turn on the oven — it tried to blow the entire room to pieces. It told the oven to release a huge volume of gas, then to ignite. It was deliberate."

Robin resets the "big red button" then waves up some log files, sharing them with Araci.

"Here. Right here," Robin points at a paragraph in the narrative log. "The AI decides it's being reverse-engineered. It knows what's going on — someone programmed it to watch for this. It's trying to self-destruct, just like a piece of military hardware might do when it winds up in enemy hands. That's a hell of a way to protect intellectual property."

"Hestia did this?" asks Araci.

"This is a Hestia meal, so yes. If Hestia gets away with it, then it becomes an industry standard. After that, AI defense of intellectual property will be pervasive."

"Isn't this all extreme?" asks Araci. "Exploding ovens are going to attract attention. That would be a publicity nightmare. Not to mention liability."

"You'd think so," says Robin. "But we're talking about AI. Not linear algorithms. You never know what the AI layers and nodes are doing. It might act when it decides it's being reverse engineered. It's just as possible the AI could decide to terminate because a location doesn't have solid IP laws. Or who knows? AIs make conclusions without human guidance. But they don't have a value for self-worth, so they can choose self-immolation as the low-cost option to protect the code."

Robin continues. "I'm speculating, but if Hestia decides it's ok for a meal to self-destruct, they might also decide it's ok for an oven to self-destruct. This oven already has simple AI for troubleshooting and self-maintenance. It wouldn't be difficult to put in a higher-level AI to detect a non-approved meal kit. You could even have two AIs — one in a rogue meal and one in the oven — and they'd be kick-boxing with each other. God help the poor schmuck standing nearby."

Araci understood. This wasn't just about Dakota anymore.

Araci MEETS the three Hestia representatives at a police target range outside of Portland. Trees surround the field — typical for Oregon. Earth berms circle the center of the field. In front of the targets is a shed with a large open door. At the shooting platform, three chairs face a table with a drape covering a cubical object.

"Thanks for joining me again," Araci begins. "Please take a seat, and I'll show you a brief demonstration that might explain some of my confusion."

The chairs are rough, but someone had the courtesy to put a water bottle on each. Lupe and another officer stand off to the side, dressed in protective gear. Araci stands in front of the chairs with his back to the table.

"Lupe and I got here a bit before you to set this up." Araci removes the drape to reveal a Hestia oven and a meal box. "I'm going to ask our officers to run this table downrange, place it in the shed, and connect power to this oven."

"We know how Hestia ovens work," asserts Broin. "Couldn't we have just sent you a promotional video?"

"This meal behaves a bit differently," replies Araci. Downrange, Lupe connects power to the oven and pushes in the meal, then both officers hustle back to the chairs.

"Let's give this a minute," says Araci. He turns to watch the table. Farj objects — but is interrupted by an explosion. The table, oven, and meal disappear in a cloud of smoke billowing out of the shed. When the air clears, only the table remains.

"The last time we met, I knew little about what Dakota was doing. I didn't realize she had an experimental Hestia meal box. But I suspect you realized that when you saw the serial number and made your abrupt exit."

Farj looks at Nilsson and Broin; Broin stares, Nilsson nervously rubs his head. They obviously discussed this between themselves already.

"This meal," Araci gestures downrange, "is like the one Dakota placed in her modified Hestia oven. We've learned it contains artificial intelligence. The explosion is what happens when one of these unknown meals talks with a Hestia oven in a diagnostic mode. The meal instructs the oven to stop attempts at reverse engineering. If the oven doesn't stop, the meal fights back. We believe this happened to Dakota Williams."

"Hestia would never instruct an AI to react like this," interjects Broin. "It's bad corporate relations, and speaking for the Hestia legal department, it's not something we would advise."

"See, that's the thing," replies Araci. "You don't tell an AI how to behave. AI chooses from options. You just provide desired endpoints. Here, a *manufacturer* — and by manufacturer, I mean *you* — only needs to instruct the AI of the problem, then sit back and let it sort out the best resolution. If you don't restrict it from a specific method, it remains a viable choice. More directly, if you don't tell it explosions are *not* an acceptable solution, then explosions remain an acceptable solution."

Farj is tapping his foot.

"Defensive AI in a meal is one thing," Araci says. "Now, let's talk about defensive AI in an oven." Araci addresses his statements directly to Farj. "If an oven were equipped with AI that obstructed competitive meals, and that oven was involved in suspicious events, well, that would be *problematic*. Do you see what I'm saying?"

Farj looks at Broin, who shakes her head *No!* The unspoken communication is clear; Hestia has already been engaged in exactly this type of project. Nilsson rubs his head with vigor; Araci could only imagine he was planning how to address this at a shareholder meeting.

"I think we understand your point," says Farj. "We are limited in our ability to discuss this at length. I assume we'll be in touch if you have other concerns."

"Actually, we will have plenty of time. I've brought along a warrant for your arrest. Something about conspiracy to defraud, but I'm sure Ms. Broin will be interested in details. Ms. Broin, I'm glad you're here; Mr. Capcin will appreciate your assistance."

Lupe escorts Farj to a waiting police vehicle, followed by Broin. Nilsson does not move, but stares downrange.

"I appreciate what you've done to make this possible," says Araci. "I hope I've lived up to your expectations. And I share your desire for Hestia to do the right thing."

"It's a costly lesson," replies Nilsson. "And I'm struggling with Dakota's death. Maybe Abundancy needs help. If I can prevent Hestia from doing this, I can block other companies from following suit."

"I don't know," responds Araci. "We humans are always looking for novel ways to kill ourselves." He stands. "I'm hungry, let's get lunch. I've heard of a new Iraqi restaurant."

"Hot Meal" is a prelude to Mark Niemann-Ross's novel, Stupid Machines, *which follows the continuing adventures of Araci Belo.*

THE GRANNY JOB

A NANSHE CHRONICLES SHORT STORY

BY JESSIE KWAK

In hindsight, it seems inevitable that Raj Demetriou would find himself standing in the walk-in refrigerator of the Bon Mirage while his client, Marta, and her quote-unquote driver interrogate a screaming assassin hanging from a chain.

An easy job, he'd thought. A simple job. A good palate cleanser after the disastrous last gig that landed him broke and with a business partner who's no longer speaking to him.

This easy job was supposed to be as a bodyguard to some breed of deep-pocketed inner planet socialite on vacation to visit her grandson. A piece of cake, given that Artemis City is one of the safest places in Durga's Belt — hiring a bodyguard here should have been a waste of money, but sweet little Marta wanted one anyway.

From the beginning, there'd been indications that something wasn't right. Raj had written them off. Take the fact that Marta traveled with her own personal driver to a planet with only a handful of private vehicles. Or the way that driver, Jirayu, kept disappearing while Marta did her sightseeing. Consider the pickpocket that targeted her in the boutique and the custodian-slash-assassin at the Terraza Gallery.

And, of course, the sharpshooter — the man now hanging in chains — who'd targeted her while she was lunching at the Bon Mirage.

Any individual moment could have been brushed off, but put them all together and the implication is crystal clear: Raj is way in over his head once again.

Goddammit.

"Ty Moxon?"

The trickle through the doors to the interplanetary passenger terminal had become a flood; Raj straightened with a bright smile at the boxy grandmother who barked out his alias du jour like an order. Client arrived, job started. As though flipping a switch, his mind had become focused and present — putting aside whatever's come before and whatever's coming next, just like was drilled into him at Mar-Alif Officer's Academy, well back before his life went to pieces three years ago.

"Yes, ma'am," Raj had said.

"Glad to see you're punctual. I hate to wait." The old woman was grandmother-shaped, but Raj wouldn't have described her as soft. Her steel gray hair curled tight against her scalp like armor, face well-lined and coppery, mouth firm-set and turned down. She'd been wearing a smart skirt suit only slightly rumpled with travel, and expensive but understated jewelry. Raj could scent her perfume over the constant undercurrent of filtered air and faint antiseptics: subtle florals with an undercurrent of spice.

"It's nice to meet you, Ms . . ."

"Marta," she'd said brusquely. "And this is Jirayu, my driver."

At the time, Raj hadn't realized she wasn't alone; a lanky middle-aged man in an unobtrusive suit skulking behind her with a neat cap of black hair and a faint smile on his thin lips that didn't make him look happy. Jirayu had given Raj an automatic nod before going back to scanning the room like a restless panther.

Raj should have found Jirayu's presence suspicious, but instead he'd been impressed: Who has the money to hire — let alone *travel with* — a private driver?

"I'm looking forward to our trip today," Marta had said, and Raj pushed the thought away. It didn't matter who she was back home. Here, she'd be his responsibility.

"Well, where to, ma'am?"

"I have a few places in mind." Sparks of humor had lit up her dark eyes. "Are you armed?"

Raj had blinked at the question, but it still hadn't raised any red flags. He had a pistol in a shoulder holster, a knife in his boot, but he never used either if he didn't need to. If it hadn't been in the contract, he would have left the gun at home.

"Yes, ma'am?"

He hadn't been able to read Marta's smile. "Good."

Marta's first stop had been Qāf Sector, a trio of interconnected platforms suspended around Level 10 of Artemis City's Bell. It's a popular spot with tourists — feels like you're floating in the middle of the giant, open space that makes up the Bell, but you can't see either the glass dome at the top of the Bell or the industrial floor that tops the enclosed levels that continue to bore deep into the core of Artemis. Most tourists never leave the Bell, and Raj doesn't blame them. He grew up with Indira's vast horizons and atmosphere — he'll never be used to the warren of cramped passages those who grew up in Durga's Belt seem comfortable with.

Different pockets of space within the Bell have different vibes. In Qāf Sector, tourists and locals alike come to see and be seen, sipping coffee and cocktails in open-air cafes, pressing their noses against the arching glass windows of the shopping arcades, strolling the walk-ways arm-in-arm and admiring the glitter of the Bell around them.

Marta stopped in at the same type of boutique Raj's mother would have frequented — these days, Raj couldn't afford a necktie from the display, never mind one of the suits. But Marta's entrance had said she had money, and both the shop keeper and a shifty young man with shaggy, blue-dyed bangs had noticed.

Raj had pretended to let his attention slip when Marta went into the dressing room, giving Shifty Bangs a chance to make a beeline towards Marta's cubicle.

Bangs'd had one hand on the door, the other pulling a knife out of his pocket when Raj clamped a hand over his mouth from behind. The kid yelped hot breath against Raj's palm, heart rate rabbiting and arms windmilling — the knife whooshed past Raj's ear, too close for comfort. Raj had slapped a tranquility patch against the side of Bangs's neck.

When Bangs went limp, Raj had wrestled him as quietly as possible into the cubicle next to Marta's, then trussed the kid's wrists and ankles and left him lying on the floor before letting himself out.

"I'd like to try this in the blue."

Adrenaline spike; Raj had whirled to Marta's cubicle to find her door cracked open, her outstretched hand holding out a green jacket with glittering buttons and bell sleeves. Raj had taken it from her without a word and stepped out of the dressing room. The attendant was staring at him, wide-eyed.

"She'd like to try this in the blue," Raj had said, handing the man the jacket and letting him know about the cleanup in cubicle three. At the time, he'd still been trying not to ruin sweet little Marta's vacation by worrying her with the pickpocket. Now, he's learned that nothing frazzles her.

Unlike Raj's mother, Marta turned out to be a quick shopper who makes firm decisions and knows what she wants. She'd chosen the blue jacket, a smart black jumpsuit, and a brightly patterned scarf. The attendant's eyes had widened when she pressed her finger to his pad to pay; whether she'd left him a tip or he recognized her name, Raj couldn't have said. The man had just bowed to them both as they left.

Now, shivering in the walk-in refrigerator, Raj would put money on the shop attendant recognizing Marta's name.

The assassin, on the other hand, is still pretending he doesn't know who he's dealing with.

"Where is he holed up at?" Marta asks again; Raj had caught a glint of fury in her eyes earlier, after the assassin's bullets narrowly missed, but now Marta's back in grandmother mode, steel curls perfectly in place. Her hands are clasped behind her, fingers of one hand tapping against the back of another in bored impatience.

The assassin grits out an answer through bloodied lips

— it sounds like "Fuck you," and Jirayu hits him once more with an electric barb. This time lasts longer than the previous ones, and when Jirayu finally lets him rest the assassin's teeth rattle like a cabinet full of heirloom porcelain in an earthquake.

Marta takes a sharp breath, annoyed. "Where. Is. My. Grandson?"

Raj's job is technically to watch the door to the walk-in refrigerator — which is something Marta would have asked him to do from the outside if she didn't want him to see exactly what she was capable of. He gets the message: You're involved now, too.

He's just still not sure *what* he's involved with.

What a surprise, he can hear Ruby saying, arms crossed and tone dry. *What a fucking surprise, Raj.*

THREE YEARS ago Raj's world imploded, and he found himself tumbling breathless and wild in one of fate's sneaker waves. If things had been a heartbeat different he would be dead; instead, he washed up in the Pearls, the dwarf planet chain in Durga's Belt, clutching fistfuls of aftermath.

Ruby Quiñones was one of the first people he met — or, at least, one of the first people he'd been able to trust. They'd quickly become business partners; they'd made a good team.

But that's all over now.

Ruby's got one of those genius hacker's minds full of meticulously filed details, and it turns out that since they started working together she's been meticulously filing away how badly he's screwed up their jobs. She'd started out tolerant of his lack of planning and slapdash approach, but the last job had pushed her over the edge. She's done with him, she'd written. Never working with him again. He hadn't believed the message at first, but she's not responding to his messages today. Not his note of apology, and not his — somewhat more desperate — note a few hours ago asking if she could help him figure out who Marta really was.

Okay, so maybe he hadn't vetted their last job as well as he should — maybe he's gotten a bit sloppy. Maybe he's gotten so trapped in the net that is his shattered life in the Pearls that he's stopped looking for a way out.

He should have known taking a job for Sara Mugisha — reigning empress of Artemis City's party scene and designer drug trade — would come with a twist. She needed some intel, she'd said; a quick freelance job to find some dirt on someone she wanted leverage over. She was willing to pay double what Raj would normally charge, and he'd talked Ruby out of her initial objections.

Only problem? The target was Kasey Aherne. Where Mugisha is the empress of the party scene, Aherne's empire is solidly blue-collar — or at least, it always had been. Turns out these days he fancies himself a refined gentleman, with a refined taste in drugs. And he owes Mugisha an obscene amount of money.

Raj doesn't care what Mugisha's plans with Aherne are — only thing he knows for certain is he took an unnecessary chance and triggered Aherne's safeguards, and Aherne will be a deadly enemy if Ruby hasn't covered their tracks good enough.

Oh. And that Mugisha doesn't pay for compromised intel.

And that Ruby still hasn't read his message asking her

to ID Marta for him; Raj slips his comm back into his pocket and turns back to the scene in front of him.

The assassin's done pretending he didn't know who Marta is, which means Raj is the only person in this tiny, frigid room who's clearly in the dark. He can hear Ruby's commentary: *I get that bodyguards are meant to keep their mouths shut, Raj. You couldn't have asked one question when she brought up family, only? Said, "Ah, your grand-son's local, that's lovely. Anyone I should know? Some self with homicidal tendency, maybe? No reason, just curious."*

At Jirayu's startled grunt, Raj straightens; the chattering of the assassin's teeth has gotten worse, and it's not just cold and electric shock. He's going into convulsions, foaming at the mouth, eyes rolling back in his head.

"For heaven's sake," Marta says crossly. She steps back, one hip bumping into a stack of boxes labeled TVP Steak. "He took poison. Jirayu!"

THE ASSASSIN in his chains was actually the third of the day.

After the pickpocket in the boutique, there'd been the fake custodian at the Terraza Gallery. Marta had wanted to go there to see a new exhibit called Trivial Influences by an artist listed as a famed zero-G sculptor from one of the Bixian settlements. The darkened gallery had been filled with a series of strange, wispy sculptures meant to illustrate "the profound loneliness and enhanced humanity of life in the deep black." An oversized hologram of ice giant Bixia Yuanjun had spun slowly against the far wall.

The custodian had shown his bad intentions towards

Marta while she was negotiating the price of one startlingly disturbing sculpture with the gallery owner. Raj had spotted him easily, and tapped the man's shoulder as he reached for something on his cart.

"Excuse me," Raj had said. "I got something on my jacket. Can I bother you for a cloth?" Raj had leaned past the man as though reaching for one of the folded cleaning cloths, and seen what the custodian was going for: a silenced pistol.

Raj had twisted sharply, swinging his elbow back to crack across the custodian's jaw. The man stumbled into the wall with a groan, and Raj grabbed him by the collar, throwing him through an open door and into an empty office.

A nearby woman in a blue suit — an office-type on her lunch break — had glanced their way in surprise. Raj shot her a bright smile. "We've got an issue with the lighting," he'd said, and closed the door behind him.

The fight had been vicious and swift, Raj's military training against the assassin's scrappy street style, and finally Raj had gotten him into a headlock. A pair of solid punches to the man's kidney dropped him to his knees; Raj caught the man's neck in the crook of his elbow, squeezing until he slumped forward.

He'd checked the custodian's pulse — still strong — and then his pockets, but he hadn't found anything besides certainty that he was a professional killer.

The woman in the blue suit had given him another glance when he let himself back out of the office, straightening his jacket and smoothing stray strands of his shoulder-length black hair back into its ponytail. But it had been more appreciation than suspicion, and she blushed when he winked.

Marta had also given him a once-over when she came out of the gallery owner's office; definitely a glimmer of suspicion there. "Is everything all right, Mr. Morgan?" she'd asked.

"It's wonderful," he'd replied. "Is everything all right with you, Marta?"

And her smile had only quirked to the side. "Splendid."

A red flag? Or just an eccentric old lady? Impossible to tell in the moment, Raj consoles himself.

After, Jirayu'd driven them to the Bon Mirage — which wasn't a red flag in and of itself. It's a cheesy tourist hotspot designed to look like an Arquellian beach resort, exactly the sort of place a grandmotherly sort on vacation to visit her grandson might choose to dine.

But once bullets started flying in the Bon Mirage's dining room, Raj quickly figured the ambiance wasn't why Jirayu had picked it. Jirayu's been on his own little murder spree with every stop they've made, knocking off high-ranking members of Kasey Aherne's organization while Raj keeps an eye on Marta. Although why Marta is sending her driver — sorry, her personal assassin — after those targets is still a mystery.

Raj isn't fooling himself that he's in this refrigerator watching the third assassin die by self-administered poison by choice. Maybe Jirayu wouldn't have let him walk away after the shootout at the Bon Mirage, but Raj could've run. He could've shot first. Could've called security.

No, he's here because Ruby's right. He sensed this job jumping the rails and instead of bailing like a sane person would do, he buckled in to see where the ride would take him. Ruby called it a death wish, but it's not a wish — it's an embrace of the inevitable. Three years ago a sneaker wave shattered Raj's life, and for all intents and purposes it killed the person he'd been. He's just been waiting for someone to put a final seal on the whole mess.

Jirayu pulls a syringe out of his jacket pocket and stabs it into the assassin's neck, but whatever magic he was hoping to pull, it's too late. The assassin gives a final shudder, then goes slack in his chains.

"Gods*dammit*." Marta exhales a sharp puff of breath into the freezing air. "I suppose we'll have to do things the hard way."

"I'm sorry, ma'am," Jirayu says, but Marta shakes her head to dismiss the apology.

"I would have expected my grandson to hire sturdier stock."

She heads for the exit and Raj pushes the door open for her politely, aware of the absurdity of the formal gesture; she's exiting a walk-in refrigerator where she just murdered the man who'd tried to kill her. The chef walking up to the refrigerator jumps when the door opens, the tray of puff pastries tilting in her hands.

"You may want to find another place to store that," Raj says to her. The chef's gaze slides past him in horror.

"Yes, my apologies," Marta says. "Please call security, we found a murderer."

Marta pats the chef kindly on the arm as she brushes past, then heads for the door, her sensible heels making soft scuffs against the self-cleaning mats on the kitchen floor. The chef nods frantically at Marta's back, her reply so faint Raj almost doesn't catch it.

She'd said, "Yes, Mrs. Aherne."

Whatever warmth was starting to work back into

Raj's body vanishes in a puff. His gaze snaps to Marta's face.

That square chin, the strong nose, broad brow always in a faint scowl — before his and Ruby's last failed job, Raj might not have known Artemis City's underworld players by sight. But now that he knows — now that he's studying Marta — he can see the resemblance. Marta tilts an eyebrow, watching this new piece of information work its way through Raj's brain.

Raj clears his throat. Pushes open the door to the street for Marta. "Ma'am? Your grandson is . . ."

"My grandson is Kasey Aherne," she says. "And he's running my business into the ground." She marches to the sedan, where Jirayu already has her door open, then pauses to study Raj. "You've more than earned your fee today, Mr. Morgan," she says to Raj. "But I will triple it if you're willing to stay by my side for the next few hours."

Raj blinks at her. She was already paying him well, and tripling that number would not only wipe out the debt he's got, but it would give him enough to lie low for a while. Take a break from the constant treadmill and figure out what's next — not just stumble into the next job, but actually come up with a plan. Do some of that soul searching Ruby seems to think he needs.

He can hear Ruby's commentary: *Now here's a great time to walk away, isn't it. Just say, "Hey man, this gig is a bit more than I signed up for," and get the hell out of there.*

But her voice is just in his imagination. Raj's comm has remained silent — Ruby still hasn't even bothered to read the message he sent her asking her to look into Marta's identity. Not that her help would have made much difference at this stage. Raj was in too deep before he ever sent that message.

Not to mention that if he sees this through the right way, he could make himself a very powerful friend.

On the other hand . . .

"I know what happens to people who bet against Kasey Aherne and lose," Raj says.

Marta smiles. "I didn't get to be as old as I am by losing."

"What's your plan?"

"I have loyal followers who still work for Kasey. Those three captains were not loyal, but I have people lined up to replace them."

"And you'll just walk into Aherne's — into your grandson's compound — and hope he doesn't shoot first?"

"Would you come with me if I said yes?"

Why the hell not, says a dark voice in his mind, and he almost says it out loud. But maybe — just maybe — he's been riding this wave out to sea long enough. It's time to start swimming back to shore.

"That would be suicide," Raj says. "But, ma'am? If I may, I have another idea."

RAJ SPINS SLOWLY in the center of the spacious warehouse, examining his work and looking for the cracks.

For the resources he has, it's not a half-bad plan.

He'd pulled in a favor with one of the dockworkers who'll still take his calls, securing them an out-of-the-way space where innocent bystanders won't get hurt if Marta's family feud comes to violence. Given the day's body count so far, it seemed smart to err on the side of caution.

The warehouse is prepped for a big shipment from a local hauler that got delayed by pirates deeper in Durga's

Belt, so there's plenty of space to maneuver and no one will be looking to bother them. A few crates are staged for loading, a forklift suit slumped dormant near the door.

Marta's sitting behind a metal table, which Raj and Jirayu dragged below one of the spotlights at the middle of the space. It's suitably dramatic, of course, but it also serves to keep the attention on her and Raj rather than whatever Jirayu may be doing in the shadows. At first glance, it might look like she's being held captive. At second glance, she's pretty clearly armed herself. He's counting on Kasey Aherne being the kind of guy who doesn't delve much beneath the surface.

"You really think he'll fall for it?"

Marta's voice echoes faintly in the silence, and Raj turns from his examination of the warehouse to face her.

"I spent the last month surveilling on your grandson," Raj says. "I might not know him as well as you do, but I know he owes Sara Mugisha a lot of money, and she's got him spooked. If he had proper time to look into his captains' deaths, he'll realize she doesn't have anything to do with that. But he's running scared. The message we faked from Mugisha claiming she's holding you hostage will get him here to talk. Then it's up to you."

"Tell me why he owes Mugisha money?"

"She runs party drugs, booze. Protections for the service industry and sex workers unions — that sort of thing. He, ah . . ." Raj realizes he's trying for delicate, but he just saw Marta torture her would-be assassin. She's not the kind of person who needs news broken to her gently. "Basically, anything she's got for sale, he's gotten himself hooked on it."

"That fucking idiot."

Raj glances down at her, trying to make out the sweet

old tourist woman he'd thought he was meeting at the terminal. Marta's mouth has a hard line to it, her papery hands folded neatly in front of her, her pistol obscured by the bell sleeve of her new blue jacket. Still, when she glances up at him her eyes hold a touch of humor, like they're in on a joke together.

He's not sure what joke they're in on, though. He's not quite her bodyguard anymore, now that he's started offering suggestions and she's started taking them. But he's not a partner, either. A warm eddy of anticipation surges through him — whatever happens after this, his life doesn't need to be a binary choice between letting himself be trapped in his family's plans, or letting the sea take him.

There's a third option. An unknown road. Taking it is terrifying as hell, but at least it'll be his choice.

"I should have come back and made things right after my son's death," Marta says. "Instead of letting Kasey make a fool of the Aherne name."

"What happened?" Raj asks.

Marta's glance is sharp, but there's an amused twist to her lips that says she doesn't mind being questioned. Not by him, anyway. Or at least not this time.

"It's every entrepreneur's dream to build a strong business that can continue to support their children," Marta says. "I retired in my prime to give my son a chance to prove himself, and to enjoy the fruit of what I'd built. My grandson, however, couldn't manage to wait for the business to become his. I heard rumors that he'd helped his father along to an early grave. A few years later, I stopped receiving the dividends I was due — so either the business was in trouble, or my grandson had lost sight of what made him successful."

"So you came back to set things straight."

Marta gives Raj a long look. "I could probably have saved a lot of trouble today if I had just asked you if you knew my grandson."

"I think we both could've saved a lot of trouble by asking questions earlier."

And there's the sweet tourist that he picked up; Marta's eyes twinkle. "Come now," she says. "You've had fun."

"It's been an interesting day."

Raj senses more than hears a change in the dock noise outside the warehouse doors. Voices gathering, orders being given. He straightens and settles a hand on Marta's shoulder. She shivers at the touch — electricity crawls over his skin, too — and turns back to the door.

"You know," she says. "I like you. If this works, I'm going to need people I can trust to help me get things back on course."

Raj hasn't kept the surprise off his face; Marta smiles faintly, then turns back to the door. His mind probes uncertainly at the idea of working for Marta Aherne. Fortunately he doesn't need to respond now, because Kasey Aherne throws open the doors.

Even in the weeks since Raj and Ruby finished their surveillance on Kasey, he's grown thinner, more antsy. His movements are jerky and unnatural, like he's either coming down from a high or working up to it. Raj wonders if he was already flying when he got the "meet us here or your grandmother is dead" note, or if he popped a pill to help him deal with the situation.

Maybe the former, because despite the note's warning to come unarmed he's brought no small amount of fire-power. Either he didn't read it well, or he doesn't really care if his grandmother gets killed by his blunder. A flare of indignation at Marta's expense blooms in Raj's chest. What kind of monster doesn't care what happens to his own granny?

Kasey Aherne strides into the warehouse, suit jacket open to reveal his shoulder holster, flanked by almost a dozen of his soldiers. Each of them is armed to the teeth, and each one of them is aiming their fury directly at Raj.

The goal is for Marta being able to talk them out of this; bar that, he's counting on her assertion that quite a few of Kasey's soldiers are still loyal to her. Raj and Marta are both armed, and Jirayu's waiting somewhere in the wings with his bag of tricks. But the odds are pretty terrible if it comes to a physical altercation.

A trickle of sweat tingles down Raj's spine; he ignores it, staying loose and ready for whatever comes. Conversation and violence aren't the only tricks up his sleeve right now, but they're the most reliable. He keeps his hand glued to Marta's shoulder, praying this works.

"What is this?" Kasey growls to Raj as his soldiers fill in behind him. He's stopped just outside the circle of light; they'll need to draw him in.

"It's nice to see you, too, Kasey," Marta says.

Kasey blinks his attention from Raj to Marta and back. "Where's Mugisha, then?"

"I'm glad you could come," Marta says. "I trust you got my messages this morning."

Kasey frowns at her, balance thrown off by the fact that she's not acting like a hostage. "What are you talking about? I didn't know you were in town. Why didn't you tell me you were coming to visit?"

"I'm not here for a visit," Marta says. "I'm back for good."

Raj has been studying Kasey's soldiers to suss out which will break for Marta if diplomacy shatters; Marta's statement nets him some useful reactions: The woman with the black braids at Kasey's side straightens, her weapon lowering slightly. A man in a white blazer trades his scowl for a look Raj might read as hopeful. The pair watching the door lean in to whisper; one casts an unabashed glare at Kasey's back.

"You're working with Mugisha?" Kasey asks his grandmother.

"Of course not."

Kasey points a finger at Raj. "That man works for her," he says, and Raj winces — apparently Ruby wasn't able to cover their tracks after all. "He's one of her goddamned spies, isn't he."

"Wrong," snaps Marta. Kasey's spine straightens involuntarily at the rebuke. "He was working for me to get information on you. I kept hearing how bad things had gotten here, and I needed to know for myself before I came here to set you straight."

"But Mugisha — "

"Kasey Ami Aherne, you'll listen to me." Marta's tone sharpens and Kasey glances at his people; Raj wonders if he's beginning to regret bringing them here to witness the vicious dressing down. A faint dark flush is creeping into his cheeks, and Raj doesn't get the sense Kasey's the kind of man who takes humiliation well. Kasey shifts his stance uncomfortably, stepping closer to the circle of light, but not close enough.

"You've surrounded yourself with some questionable influences," Marta continues. "I removed them. And I'm back to replace you as head of the business."

"You never let me run it my way to begin with," Kasey

snarls. "Always asking for more and more? You're siphoning off all the profits."

"The increase in amount is called *interest due*, child," Marta says impatiently. "And my dividend wouldn't have been a burden if you'd run this business with any sort of sense. When I was in charge, I certainly wasn't dissolving all our profits under my tongue for a cheap high."

People shift at that — Marta's hit a nerve, and Raj marks who shoots Kasey angry looks. Braids angles her body away from Kasey almost unconsciously. Blazer taps his palm against his thigh. The pair at the door have abandoned their post, coming forward as though to help cover Marta.

Kasey steps forward, toes nudging into the circle of light, face contorted in rage. One more step is all Raj needs out of him; he squeezes Marta's shoulder to remind her and that spark of electricity slithers over his skin once more. She lifts her chin.

"All that could be forgiven," she says. "But I'll never forgive you for killing your father."

Kasey Aherne roars back with anger — back out of the light — and aims his pistol between his grandmother's eyes. Guns snap to attention around him — but more than Raj was hoping for are trained on him and Marta. The flicker of hope in his gut sinks like a stone.

"You should have died years ago," Kasey snarls, and squeezes the trigger.

The room explodes in a concussive array of rainbow sparks, and Raj can't tell if they're real or just his skull lighting up behind his squeezed-shut eyes. A light above them shatters, raining down shards of glass, but his skin is singing with electricity and he barely feels it.

He dives for Marta before Kasey can get another shot off, mildly stunned that they're both still alive.

The experimental exploding shield is terrifying, but it worked. The tiny part of his mind that isn't preoccupied with survival is cataloging his feedback: wearing it makes your skin crawl, and it sucks all the air out of your lungs when it detonates. The thick reek of scorched skin and blood clogs his nostrils — he hopes that's an aftereffect and not a sign that he or Marta are injured.

Oh. And one more piece of feedback. The explosion didn't extend far enough to hit Kasey Aherne.

Kasey's second shot thuds into Raj's chest armor when Raj dives in front of Marta, a combination of the explosion and Kasey's drug twitches ruining his aim. Raj grunts at the impact — this is high-end stuff leftover from his Arquellian navy days, but Kasey was close.

He lets their momentum roll him and Marta behind a crate; she pushes herself into a crouch and squeezes off a pair of shots with accuracy Raj no longer finds surprising. The big man with the reddish beard — the one who was charging at their hiding spot — goes down with blood blooming on his chest.

Grandma's still got it.

"Who do I shoot?" Raj yells to Marta. His voice sounds underwater, thick; that the experimental exploding shield fucks with your hearing is another piece of feedback.

"Just cover me," she yells back.

Kasey's team is in chaos. Braids is wrestling him for his gun, but she doesn't seem to be trying to hurt him. "That's your fucking *grandmother*," she yells as another one of Kasey's men grabs her from behind. She breaks his grip and spins, punching him in the jaw, then turns to face her next attacker, a tall man with spiked purple hair. Raj's shot takes Spikes through the neck without waiting for confirmation from Marta.

"That one was good, right?" Raj asks. Marta nods and fires at a tattooed woman who's been taking potshots at them from the other side of the warehouse.

The man in the white blazer has taken out a couple more of Kasey's loyal soldiers, and soon Braids and Blazer are fighting back-to-back near the pile of crates Marta and Raj took shelter behind. They're joined by the couple who were standing back by the door — but Raj doesn't have time to dissect the shifting loyalties of the Aherne organization at the moment because Kasey himself is leaping over the pile of crates to get to them.

Raj catches him midair, angles his body so that when they hit the ground rolling, Kasey acts as his cushion. The impact still slams through his bones — he's going to need more than a nice hot shower to ease today's bruises.

Start the day putting on your nicest suit to trail a tourist around the Bell, end it by wrestling around on the floor with one of Artemis City's major crime lords. Story of his life, Raj might have said earlier today, complete with a self-deprecating laugh. Only now, he can see exactly what Ruby means. She's not willing to roll the dice on her day — she wants to know what they're getting into so she can be prepared. So she can come home each day for her brother.

Raj is starting to see the appeal.

He ducks Kasey's wild swing and sends Ruby a silent thought of apology. If he makes it out of this, he'll have a few people to do right by.

Kasey Aherne is a scrappy, vicious fighter. Raj clearly has more hand-to-hand combat training, but Kasey makes up for it with his fury — and whatever drug is currently spiking his bloodstream. The other man swipes at Raj with clawed fingers, teeth bared and snarling. Raj twists out of the way, elbow to Kasey's gut, and breaks the grip, rocking back up to a crouch. He dodges as Kasey lunges at him, yelping when Kasey's heel connects with his shin. The leg still bears weight, so Raj plants his feet and grips Kasey by the shoulders, using the momentum of his next swing to fling him past and send him crashing into a stack of crates.

The top one crashes down, the hasp shattering and spools of industrial electrical insulation spilling out over the floor of the warehouse.

"Fight's over," he calls to Kasey, who's peeling himself off the ground, teeth bloody, panting for breath. Raj spots his pistol where it landed near the table, scoops it from the floor and covers Kasey, keeping his body in between the snarling madman and Marta.

"No one wants to hurt you," Marta calls. "We're just here to help."

The fury of the fight is ebbing around them, and as far as Raj can tell Marta's loyalists have won. A few of Kasey's people are restrained, a few are lying prone on the bloody ground — precision shots through the eye suggest Jirayu. But the rest have either given up their weapons or decided to join Braids and Blazer.

Braids steps forward, making herself the de facto spokesperson of the loyalist Aherne faction. "It's good to have you back, ma'am," she says.

Marta holds her arms wide, pulling Braids in for a brief hug. "It's good to be back." She smiles at the others. "I don't recommend retirement," she says.

Blazer grins back. "I always said retirement wouldn't suit you, ma'am."

Marta turns back to her grandson. "Now. As for you —"

Kasey screams and lunges for her.

Raj aims to wound — he's still not sure how Marta will take to him killing her grandson — but when Kasey hits the ground his eyes have rolled back in his head. Panic grips Raj until he spots the tranq dart in Kasey's neck along with the bullet hole Raj put in his arm.

Jirayu.

As if summoned, Marta's "driver" appears from the shadows, rifle slung over his shoulder. Braids' eyes widen when she sees him, then she grins in greeting. Jirayu lifts his chin, a smile on his lips.

Marta straightens like a queen among her people. "Let everyone know that Marta Aherne is out of retirement," she says. She looks down her nose at her grandson, then motions for two of her new soldiers to grab him. "Let's get him back home," she says. "It's time he and I had a heart-to-heart."

Raj doesn't seem to be included in the barrage of orders Marta's barking out at her crew, so he props a hip on the corner of the table and loosens the straps of his body armor, probing gently at the spot where he took a bullet for her. Nothing's broken, but he'll have a hell of a bruise over the next few weeks — a good reminder of how this day could have ended.

This morning maybe he would have said drowning in a blaze of glory in an Artemesian warehouse was a fitting end to the short and turbulent chronicles of Raj Demetriou. Now, though, something else is tugging at his subconscious. Like the quiet, certain knowledge that the dark smudge on the horizon is land after days of floating adrift in the sea.

He pushes himself off the table and holsters his pistol. Buttons his suit jacket — which is now ruined beyond repair — with a wince. What's left of Kasey Aherne's little crew is now leaping to do Marta's bidding. Blazer's directing the cleanup of the warehouse, while Braids and Jirayu have exchanged bear hugs and are in position on either side of Marta as guards.

Looks like Raj's job as day bodyguard to sweet grandma Marta is finished, which is just fine by him.

She meets his gaze across the room as he approaches, amusement twisting her lips into a smile. Marta waves off Jirayu and Braids.

"I had a lovely day, thank you," she says.

"You're welcome, ma'am."

"Although your friend's . . . experiment could use some refinement." She rubs her arms with a tiny shiver. "I still feel like ants are crawling over my skin."

"It worked, though."

"It did. Tell her she has a buyer if she can work out the kinks." Marta tilts her head, studying him. "I don't suppose you're looking for a full-time position? It's hard to find someone who's both skilled at protection and good conversation."

Raj takes a deep breath.

Somewhere out on the horizon, that dark smudge is wavering, ready to vanish forever if Raj doesn't keep his gaze locked on it and swim that direction as hard as he possibly can. Marta's offering him stability, at least for the moment. But it's only a siren's call compared to what he actually needs.

"Thank you, ma'am, but I don't think that's for me."

"I understand. But don't be a stranger." She pats his arm. "I've already had Jirayu send the funds for today, it should be in your account."

Raj smiles and bows his head to Marta. Shakes hands with Jirayu and Braids, then lets himself out. At first he's not sure where he's headed — just, away from the complications in the shattered warehouse — but he finds himself taking the lift down from the warehousing sector to the Bell's glass observation ring. He strolls the observation ring, dodging tourists who are staring through the glass below their feet at the lattice of plazas and bridges and zipping transport, deep into the glittering neon heart of the city. Others crane their necks to look up through the glass dome that tops the Bell to where ships are maneuvering in and out of the dockyard ring. Raj can't see the stars beyond, but he knows they're there. Artemis City's observation ring is meant to make you feel that a whole world has opened up to you, but the vastness of space is full of possibilities beyond.

He's not trapped here, he realizes. Not in Artemis City, not even in the Pearls. He may have come here to hide, but that doesn't mean he has to die here in exile.

Raj pulls out his comm and swipes open Ruby's message once more. He doesn't bother writing her again — plenty of time for that later — but as he reads through her catalog of accusations they no longer sting. He'd been so focused on his outrage he'd almost missed the most important line: *Get your shit together, I mean that as your friend.*

He's still got friends out here. And he may not have a destination in mind, but he's got a direction — it's time to stop treading water and head for the shore.

Raj thumbs off his comm and grins. Around him,

tourists eddy through the ring, the lights of Artemis City glittering in their wide eyes, each one looking for their own path home.

Jessie Kwak enjoyed writing "The Granny Job" so much that she expanded it into a novella that digs deeper into Raj's history and introduces his future partner-in-crime, Lasadi.

Download that novella, Artemis City Shuffle, *for free and start out on the adventures of Raj, Lasadi, and the rest of the crew of the* Nanshe *at www.jessiekwak.com/c1-shuffle.*

FULL CORE

A SODALITY SHORT STORY

BY WADE PETERSON

THE POWER MAUL SWUNG FOR THE PIT BOT'S HEAD, its spluttering blue corona adding an ozone tang to the pit's sour miasma. The punters' din rose, stale beers sloshed, and Chance's grip tightened around the railing, sensing this could be the moment Grimthorn went down. Grimthorn stood in the maul's arc, damaged servos whining as blade arms came up a beat too slow. The maul connected, discharging into Grim's systems even as its head rebounded off the gallery's safety cage. Cheers and groans erupted; betting comps paid out and adjusted their odds, ensuring a steady flow of Confed marks into the pit's coffers.

"Idiots," Chance murmured. Pit bots didn't keep their processors in their heads like humans did. Still, losing the head's sensor suite wasn't good. It would doom the average pit bot, but Grimthorn was a veteran fighter, a true contender, not some former construction bot some halfwit had over-tuned and dubbed Atlas. Dumb name, dumber bot.

Grimthorn's telltales flashed green-green-amber:

moderate mechanical damage, but power and processor core still functional. Grimthorn staggered into the larger bot, sword arms slashing and scraping across Atlas's chest plating. Atlas swung its maul through empty air twice before its algorithms changed tactics. It dropped its maul and locked heavy manipulator arms around Grim's torso. Metal crunched, servos whined, and hydraulic lines ruptured within Grimthorn. The sword arms still flailed, traveling up and down Atlas's plating, throwing sparks that sent wisps of acrid smoke curling from the pink hydraulic fluid coating both bots.

Chance wondered if Grim's algorithms had it wrong this time. Maybe something within it was broken, or Atlas's handler had sneaked an illegal mod past the stewards. Atlas's gearboxes chattered as its manipulators reached their crushing limit. Atlas released, opting for a left armlock and further pummeling. As it did, Grimthorn dropped to the deck and pivoted, pulling Atlas with it. The constructor's arms snapped together, but not before Grimthorn heaved, sword arm spearing, tip sliding through a seam in Atlas's chest plating and continuing until Grimthorn's elbow was buried deep within Atlas's innards.

Atlas seized. Three telltales flashed across its back: red-red-red. Grimthorn withdrew an arc-flash-blackened sword and withdrew two steps before crossing its sword arms overhead.

"FULL CORE!"

The punters screamed louder, and beer rained down on the pit while paper cups bounced off the safety wire. No matter who they had been rooting for, the dumb tradition brought the crowd together at the end. Chance stepped back from the railing and headed for the service door. He wondered if the tradition had developed naturally or if it was just another ploy the pit used to sell more drinks. The pit had a lot of traditions like that, both official and unofficial. He didn't doubt some kid with more wada than sense would come along and enter a pitbot named Atlas. That, too, was tradition.

IN THE REPAIR CLOSET, Grimthorn held its head in place while Chance repaired its connections. The task was familiar to them both and the bot automatically made adjustments to its grip and positioning to give Chance the working angles he preferred.

Chance smelled Campbell before he saw him, a combination of tobacco, leather, and Altarian curry houses. Campbell subscribed to the theory that colognes and musks were the essence of a man, and he was a man of great essence. Grimthorn shifted as the man entered, angling its torso to face their mutual owner.

"Is it safe to be in here with him powered up?" Campbell asked. "Get your wires crossed and you might find yourself springing a leak."

"It's got hefty limiters on what it can do outside the pit. In here, it's just a puppy."

Campbell grunted and stepped closer, squinting at the blue crystal in Grim's torso and following the leads to the test stand displaying the inner workings of Grim's code. "How'd he do it? Comps had Atlas at a ninety-eight win chance right before the end."

"Tactile feedback and percussive mapping," Chance said, seating the last connection between Grimthorn's head and body. "He figured out the other bot's exact internal layout and found a weak armor seam. Bingo-bango, right through the core. Here." Chance keyed in a few commands into the terminal and replayed the match from Grimthorn's memory, a wireframe model of Atlasbot taking shape along with a probability map of its internal configuration.

"Nice." Campbell pursed his lips and gave him a side-long look. "You sneak it a mod?"

"That would be illegal." Both of them grinned, then Chance waved the comment away. "No mod, just experience. Grim built its blind fighting technique all by itself."

"I didn't know they could do that." Grimthorn's optic band powered up and focused on Campbell, who shifted away.

"Don't worry, it's not AI. Just some seed code and a lot of experience." He patted one of Grim's heavy-duty leg actuators. "A lot of experience."

"I had a good chunk of wada riding on a win. Thought he might lose."

"I told you it wouldn't."

"You did say that, you surely did." Campbell paced around the workbench, running fingers across scarred bot armor and wrinkling his nose as they came away coated in soot and pink fluid. Chance handed him a clean shop towel; Campbell nodded a thanks as he wiped his hands. "You see, that's what I like about you, Chance. I know you're not going to let me down. Others, they ask me what I'm doing with a vat job like you, that you're not worth all the fuss and upkeep, but I tell them you're reliable, you're like Grim here. Old, but experienced."

"I've always appreciated our arrangement," Chance said. It never hurt keeping your full-spec patron happy, especially one who had his sigil tattooed on your neck.

Campbell's mark was as good as power armor on Backside Station, where stumbling across a dead clone was one of the more routine annoyances. Even other full-spec humans paid Chance a modicum of respect by proxy once they noticed it.

"We've made some money together, haven't we?"

"Good business, good life, a wise man once said."

Campbell smiled, knowing damn well it was one of his favorite sayings. "Got you something." Campbell reached inside his jacket and Chance's chest twinged. He didn't have any reason to think Campbell would pull the beamer from its shoulder holster and put a hole through his chest, but it was always a possibility.

In the earlier days, when Campbell was just small-time, Chance and another clone had been in one of the quieter loading bays with the man, playing cards while waiting for an overdue smuggler. Campbell had sneezed mid-game and reached into his battered leather jacket, but instead of pulling out a tissue, out came the beamer. Bam. One more dead clone for the recyclers, and the lingering smell of burnt meat. Chance never forgot the confused look on the clone's face. Campbell had holstered the beamer and shrugged at Chance's unasked question. "Long story" was all he'd offered.

Campbell's hand came out with a bottle of pills. He gave them a shake and pretended to read the label. Chance's mouth watered. He could eat a burger tonight. He would eat a burger tonight. "You're what, seventeen standard now?" Campbell asked.

"Close enough." Off-market clone brokers weren't known for their attention to detail or quality control in their products. For example, noticing the Bardos-alpha thirty-eight genetic line stopped producing critical digestive enzymes around twelve years of age. And why would they? In the Confederation, BA-38's like Chance rarely made it past middle age. For some reason, Campbell opted to keep Chance supplied and alive when a young replacement would have been cheaper.

"You ever think about what to do after all this? Like retire, maybe get a couple of vat jobs yourself, you know, to take care of you?"

Chance ducked his head and shrugged. "I've been saving by. Found a nice place on the station's planetside that should open up in a few months."

"Saving by, that's a good way of putting it." Campbell looked around the repair closet and sighed. "You got it easy, Chance. I gotta keep up keeping up, you know? Clothes, memberships, just had to get rid of my system hopper and upgrade to a punch ship so no one in the Cairo system forgets about me. Price of responsibility." He hefted the pill bottle. "Which reminds me. I need one of your special serums."

"Of course, bossman. What model and what round?"

Campbell nodded at Grimthorn. "I need him to go down in the third."

Chance felt a void growing in his belly. It had to come sometime, he knew. He had just been hoping Grimthorn was more valuable as a contender than a quick score. But as the void gnawed away, Chance's head could only move in one direction when the boss gave an order. "Okay, I can do that."

"Full core, Chance."

Chance pressed his lips together, trying to find the right words. "I can't guarantee that. If his next fight is against one of those wannabes like tonight, it might only be a disablement."

"It won't. I'll take care of the card, you mind your end." He shook the pill bottle and tossed it to Chance. "Got it?"

He pocketed the bottle, no longer hungry. "Got it, bossman."

THE PIT's arbiters were as close to AI as allowed in Confederation space: smart, thorough, and idiot-proof, but Chance had always been the better idiot. A year after he started servicing Campbell's pit bots, he forgot to sterilize the hydraulic line on a lightweight fighter and it had gone in the pits circulating repair nano meant for another model. After taking a few hits, the incompatible repairs and subverted pressure sensors slowed and confused the bot's combat routines, and it walked straight into a tungsten claw strike. Later, Chance realized his mistake while also learning the arbiters only looked at a bot's processor code and frame components, which included the hydraulics, but not the fluid. After some experimentation, Chance had perfected his serum, a specialized mix of timed nanos that caused a system disruption. Not much, just enough to throw a bot's timing off.

Chance filled a vial with a dose of serum and chased it with ten cc's of pink hydraulic fluid. "You had a good run, Grim, but it had to end sometime, right?"

Grim watched him as he dumped it into its hydraulic reservoir, then back at him. Grim had no facial expression, of course, but the tilt of its head sent a stab of guilt through Chance's belly, or was it just his pancreas?

"Hey, one for you, one for me, eh?" Chance shook out a pill and dry swallowed it. "Don't look at me like that.

You know what I meant. Eventually someone with more money than brains gonna sponsor a ringer, a real combat bot, not an overclocked civilian job and then where would you be? Where would I be? Better this way, so's maybe only one of us ends up dead when bossman comes round asking the tough questions. Can't fight it, it's just business."

⸻ ✳ ⸻

Chance watched the gates roll up and spat on the deck. A beefed-up security chassis stood across the way, a broad-shouldered riot-control model in gleaming white ceramic armor with a chimera rod in place of a stun baton. Coremonger looked impressive, but Chance recognized it for what it was: a chump. A puffer. Security bots had combat progs, sure, but optimized for group actions and humans, not pit fighting. They did well enough in early matches but never rose above mid-tiers. Everybody knew this, even the drunkest punters in the back rows. But while many looked confused, they took out their squares and placed bets like good little degenerates.

Chance found Campbell's grinning face in a luxury box and wondered if he was counting his money already. He would build this chumpbot up, fix a few more matches, and when the odds were ripe, send it to the slaughter. Another one of the pit's traditions. Chance looked away and kicked at a cage post. Grimthorn deserved better.

The first round started and Grimthorn ran its opening subroutine, angling its blades through whirling patterns while contorting itself through moves impossible had its android body been limited to human motion. Feints, strikes, and blocks all mapped against a security frame's baseline, building an updated model of its opponent. The security bot ran through routines of its own, though with a more aggressive bent. It kept the chimera in its meter-long club form, trying to overwhelm with power strikes and relying on its heavy armor to absorb Grimthorn's counters. The blows never landed squarely, if at all, Grimthorn constantly moving, darting, feinting, and countering. As time ran out, Coremonger changed chimera modes, memory metal unfolding and thinning into a long blade with an elongated hilt, a hand-and-a-halfer. Coremonger swung but Grimthorn stepped under and pushed the secbot off balance, following with a thrust into Coremonger's left elbow and severing a servo feedback cable. Coremonger's left hand spasmed and locked.

"Clever boy," Chance muttered. The chimera had many modes, but the hand-and-a-half blade was the least favorable config for Grimthorn's fighting style. By taking a hand away, Coremonger wouldn't be able to use it as an effective two-handed weapon.

The buzzer sounded, and the bots went to their corners where the pit's automated repair heads went to work in a shower of sparks and flashes of spot-welding. Chance watched as Grimthorn's left knee glitched, a stutter almost too quick to notice but confirmation the serum's nanos had activated.

The buzzer sounded again to start the second round and with the first step, Grimthorn knew something was wrong. It froze after its first step and rather than ducking under Coremonger's charge, it shuffled to the side and took a glancing blow. Grim launched a counterstrike that missed an armor seam and chattered across Coremonger's plating, an ineffective blow despite throwing sparks the punters all went wild for. The round degenerated from there, Grimthorn on the defensive, taking damage while trading blows with Coremonger, an attrition battle it could not hope to win. Had it not taken out Coremonger's left arm, the match would have ended there.

When the buzzer sounded, Grimthorn's telltales winked amber-green-amber. Repair heads worked, leaving glowing seam welds snaking across its battered armor. The right sword-arm had lost its tip. The bot's optic band turned its focus on him, and he had to look away. Nothing he could do. He searched for Campbell's face even though he knew he shouldn't. If some punter noticed through the beer buzz and made a connection . . . Clones had been killed for less, and a protection tattoo was no use against mobs.

The buzzer sounded, and the bots rose on whining servos. Chance wanted to walk away, but forced himself to watch the slaughter. The crowd had to know it was coming, even with their beer-buzzed brains. Grimthorn knew. Even Coremonger's dim programming had noted something, for it had changed its chimera's memory metal from blade to a two-tongued flexi-whip. It lashed out, aiming for an exposed limb. Grimthorn guarded itself high and low, angling its blades to deflect the whip's questing tongues. Whether because of the serum's inter-ference or mechanical damage, a few centimeters' gap soon opened in Grim's guard, though it may as well have been a kilometer. Coremonger sent the whip through the gap, and twin tongues wrapped around Grimthorn's leading wrist. Coremonger yanked Grimthorn to the floor.

Coremonger raised a heavy leg. The crowd held its breath, a few remembering Grim's previous bout, but the leg drove down, crumpling Grimthorn's torso. There was no miraculous spear from below; there couldn't be with the serum sending conflicting signals through Grimthorn's frame. But somehow the bot kept fighting.

Grimthorn pushed with sword arms, trying to rise. The crowd erupted, shouting and swearing, and Chance wondered if the veteran had anything left, some hidden subroutine kept in reserve. Coremonger stomped again. Metal crumpled. Grimthorn's arms splayed and blue smoke billowed from an overloaded shoulder servo. Grimthorn gathered itself again only to flatten under a third stomp that cracked armor seams and exposed its inner frame and wiring. A hydraulic line burst and painted Coremonger's leg pink. Grimthorn lay motionless, telltales flashing red-amber-red. The chimera's whips coiled and compressed themselves into a new configuration: an armor-piercing spear.

The match was over; why wasn't the arbiter ending it? Chance waved his hands at the arbiter's sensor cluster mounted high in the pit's rafters. "Call it! Call it!"

The spearpoint scraped along Grimthorn's back, riling up the punters into a froth as it traveled towards Grim's processing core. There the tip stopped and Coremonger drew its arm back, preparing for the core strike. Chance clapped hands over his ears against the din, unable to look away, unable to control a gut that wouldn't unclench no matter how much he repeated, "it's just business" over and over in his head.

Coremonger's arm servos whined, driving the chimera. Grimthorn bucked one last time, fouling Coremonger's aim, the spear tip penetrating Grimthorn's armor where a human might have kidneys, where pitbots kept their power cells. The cells were tough, meant to survive being pierced, crushed, and burned without discharging. The power cables leading from the cell stack, coated in the same hydraulic fluid covering both fighters, were a different matter.

A great flash blinded Chance, and heat rolled over his face. Klaxons sounded, and the pit's arbiter immediately flooded the pit with fire retardants. The crowd shifted like a startled animal but soon collected itself as it realized it was in no danger. The stench of cooked electronics mixed with melted plastic and metal slag filled the air, refusing to leave even as the pit's exhaust fans kicked over to full power. Chance blinked away purple afterimages and struggled to make sense of the scene emerging before him: two charred heaps covered in retardant snow, one large, the other with a chimera rod fused to its backplate. The blackened telltales on each winked red-amber-red: disabled but cores intact.

"Double mobility kill. Match draw." said the arbiter's vocoder.

Beer foam rained down on the metal invalids, and two tractor-treaded tenders rolled into the pits to take the remains away. Chance caught himself smiling, but quickly schooled his face and looked up. Campbell was gone.

CHANCE MANAGED to stabilize Grimthorn's power feed and get the bot sitting up, but its frame was a total loss. He might salvage a few servos, perhaps a sensor or two, but he wouldn't trust the bot to make it across the room in one piece. Still, the processing core had survived, proving that even soulless automatons could get lucky. If only it applied to clones too.

The musk hit him and his skin went cold. Fabric rustled behind him and he turned to find Campbell in the doorway, staring through him with arms folded.

"Tell me what happened," Campbell said. His dead stare slid to rest on Grimthorn's frame.

"The serum took, you saw."

"What I saw was not what I specified." Campbell's voice tightened as he drew out the last syllables. "I specified a full core in the third, and what I got instead was the worst possible outcome: two wrecked fighters and a push. I think you've lost your touch, Chance."

"The serum isn't a precise thing, bossman. I take it too far, the arbiters are going to take notice. It was just bad luck."

"We're past excuses, Chance." Campbell took two quick steps and was suddenly looming over him.

"Grim is still a great fighter, we could — "

"Grimthorn's lost his shine in more ways than one," Campbell said, reaching past Chance and running a finger across Grim's armor. He rubbed the black residue between finger and thumb. "Ain't never gonna get those odds again. Ain't worth the ducats to fix either bot." A blackened thumb pressed between Chance's eyes and left a greasy smear.

"I can make this good. Grim's core's still good. Put it in a new chassis, you'd have an instant contender once it got used to the new proprioception and kinesthetic models . . ." Campbell's hand drifted to his jacket. Chance pushed the words past the growing lump in his throat. "Even better, a stealth contender, no one would have to know."

Campbell's hand paused and instead drummed on his chest as he thought it over before shaking his head. "You had me there, Chance, you really did, but your timing's awful. I need the wada now. The game's bigger than it was back on the docks and it needs a certain amount of upkeep. I needed that payday, Chance, and you disappointed me." Campbell drew the beamer.

Promises and lies flooded Chance's brain but couldn't make it past his tongue. All these years he had known it would end like this, and now the details were filling themselves in: the scratches on the floor, the ticking of the degreaser station as it cycled, the smell of his own fear cutting through Campbell's musk. All that talk about retiring and finding a nice place and getting clone servants of his own was just that. Maybe he had lived a bit longer than the average vat job, maybe a lot longer, but it still didn't seem fair.

"Yeah, I can see why you'd think so," Chance said. "Lemme ask you one question?"

Campbell tilted his head. "All right."

"Would it have ended like this if I were full-spec?"

"Just the details, Chance, just the details. Now turn around."

"I'm fine like this."

Campbell gestured with the gun. "Around."

Chance turned, wondering why he did. What did it matter if he disobeyed now? But if he hadn't turned, he would have missed what happened next.

Grimthorn lurched as the beamer's pre-charge whirred. The gun went off, its beam singing Chance's ear and melting a hole through Grimthorn's head. Grimthorn managed a step, sword arm extended, and the beamer fired again. Something wet fell behind him, followed by a crashing Grimthorn.

Chance looked over his shoulder, his eyes quickly averting from the red mess behind him and focusing on Grim instead. Campbell's second shot had holed the torso, and Grimthorn's telltales winked red-red-red and fading. The beam had obliterated Chance's earlier repairs and winged the processor besides, its blue crystal hazy and cracked along one edge. Chance pulled it from its cradle, heat searing his fingers as he set it in the test rig.

"Stay with me, champ. Stay with me..."

The rig cycled and Chance cleared away the errors, bypassing the main boot sequence and going right into diagnostic mode.

Grimthorn's brain was a mess, but it held together. Chance hit a few keys, and a smile spread over his face as he read the diagnostic logs. There it was, a subroutine the bot had somehow kept hidden even from his handler.

"You magnificent bastard, you bypassed your own limiters."

Did that mean it was AI? How had it ignored its own programming and chosen something else? The answer was somewhere inside that convoluted and scrambled code, if he could puzzle it out.

The ticking of the parts washer snapped him out of his fugue, and he noted a smell he didn't want to identify coating the back of his throat. Time for philosophy later. Campbell's tattoo would be worse than no protection at all once word got out. Backside Station wasn't big enough to hide a clone on the run; he needed to put a few parsecs between himself and Campbell's replacement.

Chance stayed in the repair closet long enough to decouple Grim's sword arm, retch into the recycler twice, and run his hands through three washes in the degreaser station. He left with Grimthorn's processor and Campbell's square containing the access codes to his ship, along with the thumb that unlocked it.

The galaxy was a big place; big enough for a clone, a pitbot core, and a jump ship to get by if they were clever enough to change their programming.

Wade Peterson is currently working on a full-length series set in the Sodality. For more adventure, check out Wade's Badlands series by downloading Black Betty, a Badlands story, for free at www.wadepeterson.com/signup.

GREG DRAGON

Greg Dragon brings a fresh perspective to fiction by telling human stories of life, love, and relationships in a science fiction setting. This unconventional author spins his celestial scenes from an imagination nurtured from being an avid reader himself. His exposure to multiple cultures, religions, martial arts, and travel lends a unique dynamic to his stories. You can enjoy excerpts from his work by visiting his website.

Twitter: @hobdragon
Facebook: facebook.com/anstractor
Website: gregdragon.com

BENJAMIN GORMAN

Benjamin Gorman is an award-winning high school English teacher, political activist, author, poet, and co-publisher at Not a Pipe Publishing. He lives in Independence, Oregon with bibliophile and guillotine aficionado Chrystal, his favorite son, Noah, and his dog, E.V. (External Validation).

His novels are *The Sum of Our Gods, Corporate High School, The Digital Storm: A Science Fiction Reimagining of William Shakespeare's The Tempest,* and *Don't Read*

This Book. His first book of poetry, *When She Leaves Me*, was published in November of 2020, and his second, *This Uneven Universe*, will be released in November of 2021. He believes in his students and the future they'll create if given the chance.

Twitter: @teachergorman
Instagram: @teachergorman
Facebook: facebook.com/TeacherGorman
Website: teachergorman.com

JESSIE KWAK

Jessie Kwak has always lived in imaginary lands, from Arrakis and Ankh-Morpork to Earthsea, Tatooine, and now Portland, Oregon. As a writer, she sends readers on their own journeys to immersive worlds filled with fascinating characters, gunfights, explosions, and dinner parties. When she's not raving about her latest favorite sci-fi series to her friends, she can be found sewing, mountain biking, or out exploring new worlds both at home and abroad.

She is the author of supernatural thriller *From Earth and Bone*, the Bulari Saga series of gangster sci-fi novels, the Nanshe Chronicles series of space pirate adventures, and productivity guide *From Chaos to Creativity*.

Twitter: @jkwak
Instagram: @kwakjessie
Facebook: facebook.com/jessiekwak
Website: jessiekwak.com

MARK NIEMANN-ROSS

Mark Niemann-Ross is an author, educator, and chicken wrangler living in Portland, Oregon. He teaches "R" — a programming language, and "Raspberry Pi" — a small computer used for the Internet of Things. Both topics influence his writing, which fits solidly in the genre of "Hard Science Fiction."

Mark co-authored his first story in 2005 with Richard A. Lovett in *Analog, Science Fiction and Fact*. Since then, he has published additional stories in *Analog* and *Stupefying Stories*, has self-published two collections, and collaborated on a children's book.

Most recently, Mark published *Stupid Machine*, a science fiction murder mystery solved by a refrigerator.

Mark lives in Portland, Oregon. He does not have cats because his chickens would object.

LinkedIn: linkedin.com/in/markniemannross
Twitter: @marknr
Goodreads: goodreads.com/niemann-ross
Website: niemannross.com

WADE PETERSON

Wade Peterson is the author of the Badlands Born series and lives in Dallas, Texas. His stories have received honorable mentions in the Writers of the Future contest and are available online and on his website.

When not writing, he's in the back yard trying to master the arcane mysteries of Texas barbecue while also wrangling his over-scheduled teenagers, serving the whims of two passive-aggressive cats, and agreeing with whatever wine his wife pairs with dinner.

Twitter: @w_peterson
Instagram: @realwadepeterson
Facebook: facebook.com/realwadepeterson
Website: wadepeterson.com

KATE SHEERAN SWED

Kate Sheeran Swed loves hot chocolate, plastic dinosaurs, and airplane tickets. She has trekked along the Inca Trail to Macchu Picchu, hiked on the Mýrdalsjökull glacier in Iceland, and climbed the ruins of Masada to watch the sunrise over the Dead Sea. After growing up in New Hampshire, she completed degrees in music at the University of Maine and Ithaca College, then moved to New York City. She currently lives in New York's capital region with her husband and two kids, plus a pair of cats who were named after movie dogs (Benji and Beethoven).

Her stories have appeared in publications such as Fireside Fiction, the Young Explorer's Adventure Guide Volume 5, Electric Spec, and Daily Science Fiction. She's the author of the *League of Independent Operatives* superhero series and the *Toccata System* sci-fi novella trilogy.

Website: katesheeranswed.com

MARK TEPPO

Mark Teppo divides his time between Portland and Sumner, and he tends to navigate by local bookstore positioning. He writes historical fiction, fantasy, speculative fiction, and horror, and has published more than a dozen novels. If he's writing a mystery, he's pretending to be Harry Bryant.

He also runs Underland Press, an independent publishing house.

Twitter: @markteppo
Instagram: @mark.teppo
Website: markteppo.com

ERIC WARREN

Bestselling author Eric Warren has loved stories all his life. And despite writing from a young age, it took him a few years to realize being an author was what he wanted to do for a living.

Today, he is the author of over twenty novels, including the highly successful INFINITY'S END series. Never one to shy away from what he loves, he plans to continue writing for another century, depending on the viability of life-extending technology.

He currently resides in Charlotte, NC, with his very patient wife and one small pug. Find him at ericwarrenauthor.com to keep up with all his new releases and exclusives.

Facebook: facebook.com/ericwarrenauthor
Instagram: @ericwarrenauthor
Website: ericwarrenauthor.com

LOOKING FOR MORE GREAT
SCI-FI CRIME READS?

HEAD TO
*JESSIEKWAK.COM/
BAD-INTENTIONS*

BAD INTENTIONS PRESS

CPSIA information can be obtained
at www.ICGtesting.com
Printed in the USA
BVHW071203051021
618194BV00002B/43